The Civil War in Roswell, GA

...and the Ghosts It Left Behind

A Collection of Short Stories

The Civil War in Roswell, GA

...and the Ghosts It Left Behind

A Collection of Short Stories

Connie M. Treloar

fW Publishing / Marietta GA

The Civil War in Roswell, GA.
All Rights Reserved Copyright ©2007
Connie M. Treloar

The Archibald Smith Plantation, Roswell, GA
Cover Photo by Connie M. Treloar

For Information, please address:
FirstWorks Publishing Co., Inc.
P.O. Box 93 / Marietta, GA 30061-0093
Email: firstworks@mindspring.com
website: www.firstworkspublishing.us

Cover Design by Audra Pettyjohn, Graphic Artist
Evolution Designs, Dawsonville, GA

Library of Congress Control Number 2007930665

ISBN: 978-0-9716158-5-4

Printed in the United States of America

Dedication

This book is dedicated to my husband, Steve. Thank you for your endless support and patience, and for being the wonderful partner, friend and father you are. And, while I am still "warm," may you never doubt my love...

A Word from the Author...

Few can deny that over the centuries ghost stories have intrigued the masses. Shakespeare wrote his own version in "Hamlet" and early American folklorists incorporated phantoms within their stories. Before I was twelve years old, I must have read every ghost book there was on the shelves of the Hunt Branch Library in my hometown of Fullerton, California. When my family and I relocated to the South, there was no escaping the lure of its history and the horrors of war that ravaged its soul, all of which rekindled my fascination with hauntings that were occurring in Roswell. It has been said that the energy of "supernatural phenomenon" can be attributed to events of extreme emotion—anger, sadness, horror, and loss.

No other milestone in our American history has had a greater impact on her humanity than the Civil War. Historians have recorded that the September 17, 1862, Battle of Antietam, in Maryland, is considered to have been the bloodiest single day of fighting in U.S. history. It resulted in 23,000 Union and Confederate dead or wounded— approximately nine times that of the June 6, 1944 D-day invasion during World War II. There were more dead and wounded at the Battle of Antietam than during the Revolutionary War, the War of 1812, the Mexican War, and the Spanish-American War *combined.*

When eleven Southern States declared their right to secede from—and then severed their ties with—the Union, that act precipitated the amputation of loved one, from loved one. A great passion not only drove the American armies on the field of battle, but on the home front as well. Civilians suffered from hunger; women worked themselves to death, and the displaced—black as well as white— wandered from town to town and state to state in search of safe haven.

The little town of Roswell, Georgia, had its own role to play during the Civil War. The town's mills provided much needed tenting and rope, as well as the material known as "Roswell Grey" for uniforms and blanketing for the Confederate Army. Union General William T. Sherman directed his cavalry, under General Kenner Garrard, to the town of Roswell to find a means of crossing the Chattahoochee River. Immediately following his arrival in Roswell, General Garrard destroyed the mills as "instruments of the Rebel cause."

The *effect* of the Union occupation upon the town's people did not end with the departure of their army. During the 143 years that followed, evidence of the War's imprint can still be found in Historic Roswell. If one but looks a little closer, some of that evidence may only be sensed, while others will dispute that the "evidence" escapes even the closest scrutiny—but then, only those who have experienced an *up close and personal event* are in a position to know for sure.

"Truth is stranger than Fiction" and, at times, it can be difficult to separate fact from fantasy. As I wrote the stories you are about to read, my intent was to entertain but, also, to weave fiction so tightly with historical fact that you, my reader, may endeavor to accept my challenge to discern that which is Truth from that which is Fiction.

If you accept my challenge, I will be honored to hear from you...

Connie M. Treloar — June, 2007

www.cmtreloar.com

Ghosts seem harder to please than we are; it is as though they haunted for haunting's sake— much as we relive, brood, and smoulder over our pasts.

—Elizabeth Bowen (1899–1973)—
From preface to *The Second Ghost Book.*

The Fog

I have wonderful and vivid memories of my great-granddaddy. They began when I was a little boy in short pants. I was twelve years old when he died. It was December 6, 1941, the eve of Japan's attack on Pearl Harbor that catapulted us into World War II.

He would sit me in his lap and settle back into his rocking chair on the front porch. I loved the smell of tobacco that drifted from the folds of his soft, worn plaid shirt, and the feel of his raspy whiskers on my cheek. I remember trying to count the hairs growing on the edge of his ear as he slowly rocked his old chair, looking out to the odd chicken running about – he had wrung the neck of "Old Sherman," the red rooster that used to chase me and my baby sister around the yard. Sometimes, great-granddaddy would stroke my hair as he told me stories. Most times, it was hard for me to stay awake, what with all that rocking going on!

I remember him telling me "It was an early and cold fall that third year of the war. The woods surrounding the little mill town of Roswell, Georgia, were carpeted with maple and oak leaves that made it a pleasant place to hide—and lie in wait. The bite of a brisk wind ushered in the mornings while afternoons were filled with bone-penetrating sunshine," he said, and shifted me to his other leg.

"Our Yankee forces had occupied Roswell, north of Atlanta,, prior to General William T. Sherman's two-month summer assault on the South's hub city. Everyone in the North knew how critical it was to capture Atlanta—to destroy their rail lines and stop the Confederates' trains that carried war materiel and foodstuffs to their armies. When the cavalry raids by Stoneman, McCook and McPherson failed to cut off Atlanta from her rail lines, Sherman resorted to a steady, nerve-wracking bombardment on Atlanta," he rubbed the tip of his nose, "Atlanta finally fell on September 2, 1864," he said and gazed out across the farm's newly plowed earth.

Despite all the action south of Atlanta and Sherman's march to the sea, great-granddaddy's small company was assigned to *keep the peace* north of the fallen city. He was a Yankee private who had volunteered for picket duty,

"Hell! It was the safest thing a Yank could do," he said, somehow enlivened by his memories. "So, there I was, sitting with my blue kepi low over my eyes—that way no one could tell whether I was napping or watching my surroundings," he said with a chuckle. "I sneaked up on that Johnny Reb across the field who, I guessed, was attached to the Confederate forces under General John Bell Hood, or maybe a deserter. That 'ol John-B Hood was somethin' else—he wasn't anything like that Reb General, Joe E. Johnston, who gave us quite a run all the way from Tennessee. We heard Hood was high tailin' it north, after he *finally* departed Atlanta," he chuckled, in the pride and delight of the memory. "Where was I? Oh, yes. To tell the truth, I almost missed spotting that Rebel dressed in his long, dun colored duster over a homespun blouse and trousers. Generally speaking, those scouts were supposed to spy out the enemy—but, there he was, lying stealth-like, almost invisible in that pile of leaves in the woods. I made my own post real comfortable. There was a pine tree, really two pines that had grown together, that I liked to set under. It had a nice wide and flat spot on the trunk to rest my back against. I spent hours watching and listening, and daydreaming about my girl—your great-grandmother—back home in Indianapolis, Indiana." He took the greatest delight in that memory. "She was so worried she'd be an old maid; and her only a gal of fifteen when I left her in sixty-one." Again he laughed.

"I watched that Johnny Reb reconnoitering his surroundings that morning; then he sat back on his haunches beside his fire of no-account kindling. He wasn't much of a scout; he liked to talk to himself. A man could hear him a mile off," he said, and slapped his free knee.

"That fool! I'd sure like that damn fool of a quartermaster to drink this mess he calls coffee," I heard Johnny Reb say. *"The only thing you're good fer is warmin' my frozen hands, you worthless spit!"*

* * * *

Three mornings in a row, the Confederate scout had observed the Yankee soldier at his post, no more than fifty yards away from his own lookout. On the fourth morning, their roles became something else.

The Yank called out, "Hey Reb, you there?"

"You know I am, Yank."

"Fine mornin' this day," the Yankee said.

"Yup, 'tis that," the Reb answered.

"A man would like a good cup of coffee, on a morning like this."

"A man would at that," the Reb replied.

"Would that man like to share his fire?"

"Ah 'spect ah could," the Confederate said.

The Yank moved low and slow, picking his way through the tall grass to the Rebel's position. He set his rifle on the ground opposite the small fire and knelt down. "I'm gonna reach into my haversack, Reb, and get that coffee."

"Jes so's you do it real slow," he answered, his hand resting on his Colt revolver.

The Yank smiled. "You bet." He dumped a handful of ground coffee mixed with sugar into the boiling water in the Reb's coffee pot.

They sat in silence, staring at the other and holding their cold reddened hands to the flame that separated them.

Pleasure flooded the Rebel's face with his first sip of real coffee *and* sugar—it had been nearly two years since he had either one. "A spot of milk would near about make this perfect, Yank," he said.

"Why don't you call me Billy?"

The Rebel laughed. "Much obliged, *Billy*," he said and shook his head. "And you can call me *Johnny*."

It was Billy's turn to laugh. "*Johnny* Reb, how 'bout that."

"How old you be, Billy?"

"I'll be nineteen, day after Christmas. How 'bout you, Johnny?"

"I guess I'm the old man here... I'm twenty-one."

That was the start of their mornings with coffee and small talk; they never discussed the war, commenting mostly on the weather or a particularly interesting creature they had seen in the forest. After an hour or so, they parted, each going about his own business—watching, listening, and waiting.

One morning, Johnny did not answer Billy's "halloo" across the clearing. At the risk of being discovered, Billy called out again. Still no reply.

When the third morning of silence came, Billy decided to go see if he could determine Johnny's whereabouts. He found the Reb lying on his side, shivering and clutching his duster about his slight body, as he lay next to the pit where his fire once burned. His face was drawn with tinges of blue about the edges and, when Billy reached out to feel his forehead, the young Rebel recoiled and whimpered, shrinking from the hand that offered assistance.

"Ah, Reb, this won't do," Billy said, taking off his blue wool overcoat and tightly packing it around Johnny. He started a fire and got the coffee going. When it had finally brewed, he placed bits of soft new bread into Johnny's mouth, followed by sips of coffee.

Johnny looked up at Billy with fever-filled eyes. "Thanks, Billy," he whispered before falling into a fitful sleep.

Billy made his way back to his position and managed to check up on the Rebel scout a few more times that day. He made Johnny drink the fresh creek water he fetched and coaxed him to eat some bread. By nightfall, Johnny fell into a deep sleep and Billy was satisfied that his friendly enemy was on the mend.

"You were one sorry-sad fella yesterday," Billy said over coffee the next morning. "I thought you were a goner."

"What's one less Reb," Johnny rasped out.

"I guess I consider you a friend after all the mornings we shared coffee. I jes' figured you might consider me the same, is all."

Johnny looked down at the blue overcoat still covering him. Shame blushed his face as he held out his hand. "I thank you, Billy. You saved my life. I ain't quite pert enuff to get about, but I 'spect that'll change soon."

Billy shook his friend's hand, then slowly made his way back to his own post. He slumped down against the crux of the two coupled pines. The sun's rays warmed Billy, urging his eyes closed. Soon he was snoring.

"Private!"

Billy felt the impact of something against his leg. He looked up, shielding his eyes from the sun's bright shafts.

"I said, Attention' Private! Are you deaf?" Billy rubbed his eyes and stood up. The Confederate Captain frowned a contemptible look. "Identify yourself, Private."

"You got me. I'm a Private in the Union forces of the United States," he said, shifting his gaze to the scene unfolding across the field.

The Confederate Captain snatched the kepi off Billy's head and tossed it into the bushes. Billy searched the ground for his rifle—it was in the hands of a grinning Confederate Private who spat tobacco juice out the side of his mouth.

Billy looked back across the field and saw Johnny sling his rifle strap over his shoulder then thrust his hands up in the air as he started across the field towards Billy and the two Confederates who had captured him.

Johnny's movements drew the captain's eye. "Throw down and show yourself," the Captain yelled, aiming his Colt pistol in Johnny's direction. "I said, throw down, Private!"

"Yes, suh!" Johnny removed the rifle from his shoulder and heaved it into the air. It sailed up and over a patch of blackberry brambles. The brown-bearded Captain continued shouting at Johnny: "Ease up, boy! Walk my way. Keep yore hands up!"

Billy made a lunge for his own gun, but the Rebel private struck Billy in the thigh with the butt end of the rifle as Billy crashed against him then, regaining his balance, planted a direct kick into the private's privates. The young Confederate let out a blood-curdling howl and rolled to his side, trying to bring up his rifle, while fighting to hold down his lunch.

The Captain swung around to Billy, then back at Johnny who was getting closer by the second. He decided the Yank posed the greater danger and set his own pistol sight on Billy. The Captain's finger tightened on the trigger.

* * * *

As Johnny approached the clearing, a rushing, low-hanging mist advanced on the two Confederates and Billy. It raced across the open field from fifty, to thirty and, finally—in mere seconds—to within only ten yards of them. It seized and enveloped the Rebel officer first, whose look transformed into stunned horror as his arms fell to his sides; the revolver clattered to the ground. The Private, still clutching his groin, forgot his pain as he threw his hands up, trying to ward off the mysterious thing that covered him.   The mist overtook the two Rebels who appeared to have been jolted in some unnatural state, as though frozen in time within the opaque prism.

The mist hung, as if its objective had been reached, neither touching, nor threatening Billy, or Johnny who had halted his advance ten yards away from where the fog began undulating and swaying in its turbulence, as if contemplating its next move.

Billy got to his feet, unable to discern what was happening to the Captain whose mouth opened and closed as though he were a fish out of water.

"Run, Billy!" Johnny shouted.   "Run!"

Billy nodded and took off in the direction of the old town where his unit was bivouacked. At the edge of the clearing, he turned and waved back at Johnny who had remained standing and watching the fog as it slowly dissolved before his eyes.

Johnny walked weak kneed toward the other two soldiers as they slowly took possession of their senses.

"Identify yourself, Private," the Confederate Captain demanded in a quavering voice.

"And that was the last thing I heard that Rebel Captain say as I made my way back to town," great-granddaddy said, reaching into his pocket for one of his hand-rolled cigarettes. "Sure took the vinegar outta that Captain," he laughed and his shoulders responded in the delight of his long-ago memory.

* * * *

One hundred years later, very near the same spot, another soul had a run in with The Fog."

Little ten-year-old Lynn lived with her family near the junction of North Coleman and Woodstock Roads.   Most of the forest remained undisturbed, a sanctuary to hundred-year-old trees, including the "twin" pines against which Billy had napped a century earlier.

It was the end of another lazy summer, and school had just started back in session. Many of Lynn's classmates attending Roswell North Elementary School would often cut through the woods at the back of Lynn's yard and use the established path that brought them to Woodstock Road and the ball fields where they played.

On this day, Lynn began her trek along the path where the twin pines stood as proud sentinels, the bold survivors of urbanization. The moment she passed the sentries, The Fog appeared, slowly drifting down the path, mysteriously taking on the form of a human as it advanced on Lynn and, suddenly, enveloped her in its shroud, literally wrapping her within its two mystical arms. An unnatural quiet pressed against her ears. Her legs refused to move, and though she kept telling herself to run, she was completely powerless to move as she stood on shaking legs fixed to the ground.

Two wildcats, snarling with fanged white teeth, raced across the path exactly where Lynn would have been walking had the Fog not seized her within its protective embrace. One wild cat chased the other, swatting at its companion's hind legs. When the battling cats were a safe distance away from her, the mist dissolved and the spell was broken, and little Lynn was free to go.

As soon as her legs felt steady enough, Lynn ran as fast as she could back home and into her mother's arms. She babbled the story to her parents, who listened with a degree of skepticism. Their belief grew, however, when they observed just how emotionally shaken and adamant she was about what she had seen *and felt*. Lynn told them she would never walk the path again. And, she never did.

Others have encountered *The Fog*. My Great-granddaddy always thought it was an entity as old and as natural as the order of things in the universe. Some people believe it is the ghost of a Cherokee Indian who refused to let the United States government remove him from his ancestors' home.

No matter the origin, the phantom Fog is apparently still with us; a benign and even compassionate ghostly presence, protecting the good and discouraging the bad of those who venture into the woodlands of old Roswell, Georgia.

Wilmer's Match

*P*rivate Pierson Robison of the 2nd Indiana Volunteers was en-camped at the edge of town in the summer of eighteen and sixty-four. Most of the action was further south and east of Atlanta.

He had little to do, in the way of garrison duty and, Lord knows, he and his compatriots had fought hard on their march from Chatta-nooga. The little town of Roswell, Georgia, was their reprieve and, so he found himself with a lot of time on his hands. The general store was a good place to pass the time and gossip with the owner, Homer Spence.

"Much obliged for these goobers, Mr. Spence," Pierson called out as he tore into the peanut shell.

Men who traded at the store hardly noticed Pierson. Some spared a nod in the young Private's direction as they went about their business; buying small bits of tobacco or looking for information about the war in the east, or exchanging a word or two with Spence.

The women, however, were tight lipped and deliberately drew their skirts close about them when they passed Private Pierson, as though the very blue of his uniform would rub off on their patched and faded clothing, tainting it and them with the scourge of Northern aggression. They were tired women—tired of burying sons and hus-bands; tired of doing without food and other necessities and, worst of all, tired of living with no hope for a better future. Hate was all that sustained them; for it was hate that gave them courage and fortitude to put one foot in front of the other, hour by hour, and day by day. Some of the baser women spit tobacco juice in Pierson's direction, to the consternation of Spence who was then obliged to clean the smelly, amber mess off the pine floor. Not one of the fairer sex in town had so much as looked the young Yankee in the face.

"They'd just as soon stick a knife in your gut as look at you, Yank," Spence said.

The sun road high in the sky as Pierson watched the woman who, upon seeing him, hesitated in the doorway. Her crimson hair glowed halo-like, backlit by the noonday sun. He stepped aside, the better to glimpse her face and the radiant tresses that scattered about her ala-baster complexion, emphasizing high, sharply defined cheekbones. Huge sea-green eyes softened as they met Pierson's stare, which star-tled him. He took a backward step and, as he did, upset a display of fruit jars that tumbled to the floor; one escaping and rolling out the front door and onto the porch.

Spence grinned and shifted the ivory toothpick that had eminent domain at the corner of his mouth. "Mornin', Miss Dotty," he said, slowly glancing in Pierson's direction who scrambled about, retrieving the rolling jars and who, as a schoolboy would, stole quick glimpses of the pretty young, redhead.

She knelt down—stealing her own quick glance into Pierson's

eyes—picked up one of the jars, and set it on the warped counter. "I've brought a dozen eggs and two pounds of butter to pay on account," she said, plunking down her split oak basket. She looked expectantly at Spence, then over to Pierson, who stood gawking at her like a gut-punched adolescent.

An innocent smile gave way to a sudden awkwardness as Pierson felt his knees weaken. He hastily pulled the kepi off his head. "Ma'am," he stammered and surrendered to a slight bow. The rest of Pierson's encounter with Dotty passed in a haze until he heard Spence's voice.

"Miss Dotty, iffen you bring me another dozen eggs, I'll call us even—on account of you bein' the only folks here-abouts with chickens."

Miss Dotty smiled and concluded her business with Spence and walked out the door.

Pierson drifted after her, fell against the porch railing and sighed as he watched Miss Dotty march north up Main Street, looking neither right nor left. He finally found the strength to mount his mule and follow after Dotty, keeping a block's distance behind her.

The sun's rays slanted across the red clay road and danced through the pines that lined the narrow alley. He saw her turn off; waited a few moments, then tied his mule to a fallen log and crept through the woods carpeted with pine needles.

You fool, what are you doing? All she did was smile at you! You know damn well what you're doin' Pierson... He snapped a low-hanging branch and caught himself before he plunged headlong into her yard and the small cabin beyond. He moved cautiously along the perimeter, looking for a spot to observe the young woman. *Ma would be ashamed if she knew you was spying on a woman. Course, she'd be pretty mad if she knew some of the other things you've done since being in the army.*

Nearly an hour had passed before Dotty came out into the yard, moving about the hard-packed clay, feeding the chickens and tossing a stick to the collie of questionable ancestry. She leaned over and re-moved her shoes; Pierson watched, aching to look into those beautiful green eyes and see her smile.

Pierson rode his old mule to the bend in the road, hitched up the animal, and slowly made his way to the brink of the woods that bor-dered Dotty's cabin, where he waited. It had become a weekly excur-sion and then, an every-other-day occurrence. *War can't last much longer. Least, that's what they're saying... She sure is a strong little thing... prettiest woman I ever did see, too. How it would pleasure me to take her walking of an evening... Maybe she'd let me steal a kiss, too...*

On those days when Dotty ended her round of chores, Pierson would shadow her slow walk down to the creek, just beyond the slope of her property. He lay flat out, on his belly, watching Dotty bathe her feet in the cool rushing water, and took note of how she carefully pulled the hem of her dress up, midway to her calf. He loved the way she moaned as the water drove the heat and dirt from her feet and the way she cupped her long, white ringless hands and lifted the clear water to her lips. He studied the way it ran down her face, along her neck, wetting the front of her bodice. And then, she opened the hooks on the front of her blouse and splashed even more water onto her exposed skin. Pierson swallowed hard, fighting the longing that pulsed his senses.

He wiled away many an hour thinking about Dotty, daydreaming of the day the cursed war would finally be over and he could make a serious bid for her affections. *I would first get rid of this infernal uniform and buy me a real fine suit. Then, I'd ask someone, maybe Spence, to introduce her to me—that's the proper way to go about making an acquaintance... and I'd ask, very politely, "Miss Dotty, may I have the honor of calling on you one fine evening?" We'd take a walk and, Lord above, you know I'd be the proudest man to have her on my arm...*

He indulged his fantasies—until the day Spence walked him to the back of his store: "Why, Yank, that prutty lady is married," he said. "You steer clear of Dotty Beaumont and her husband, Wilmer," Spence warned. "He's 'bout six foot four or thereabouts, and a mean Sumbitch. I've seen him beat the livin' daylights outta three men at once—just 'cause they looked in Dotty's general direction," he said, shaking his head. "They say Wilmer tore off Baldy-Bob's nose with his teeth, 'cause he thought the old man had cheated him at cards," Spence said, shifting the toothpick to the other side of his mouth. "He takes his temper out on Dotty, too," Spence whispered, respecting and protecting what was left of her pride.

In spite of Spence's warning, Pierson was drawn to the cabin and his observation spot the very next day where he found Dotty at the wash tub. Surprise nearly brought him to his feet when he saw the cabin door fly open and a bowl come sailing through, exploding with a hail of grits covering the red clay earth, just inches away from Dotty. The collie ambled over and lapped up the mess.

"Dotty!" A bull-like bellow thundered from the shadowy confines of the cabin.

She dropped the heavy shirt against the washboard, squared her shoulders and took a deep breath.

"You goddamned, stupid woman, I'm calling you!"

Dotty smoothed down the bodice of her faded blue dress and slowly walked up the steps to the front door. Wilmer filled the opening, standing in stockinged feet, with a two-inch wide brown leather belt hanging from his hand. His eyes bored deep into hers.

"You 'spect me to eat cold victuals? Get your sorry-ass in heah and make me a proper breakfast!" His massive hand clamped down on her shoulder. She moaned. He lifted the belt that, suddenly, snapped and pelted her shoulder. She turned in defiance, but Wilmer grabbed her and spun her around, then pushed her inside the cabin and slammed the door shut.

Wilmer's abusive behavior stunned Pierson. He had seen a lot in war, but he had never at any time in his life witnessed that kind of an assault on a woman. He jumped to his feet, then quickly sank back to his knees. *What are you going to do, bust down the door? He'll kill you and then Dotty.* As he made his way back to the road, he could only wonder what more Wilmer would do to her.

After putting in his two days of garrison duty, Pierson went back out to the cabin. He waited in his usual spot for nearly two hours. There was no sign of life anywhere. He waited until nightfall, then slowly made his way to the barn. Wilmer's horse was gone—which meant that Wilmer was, too. He walked back to the cabin and knocked on the door. A minute passed, then two. He knocked again. A shuffling noise sounded at the battered pine door. He pushed a lock of his unruly brown hair back under his kepi.

The door creaked and Dotty spoke through the small passage between them. "What do you want?"

Pierson removed his kepi, "Ma'am, my name's Pierson Robison and I'm here to... to see if... if you're alright." He stepped back as she widened the divide between them. He saw the inch-long cut on the right side of her face and the purple finger marks on her thin, white throat.

"Whatcha you doin' snooping around here for? I'm fine, but if my husband sees you, *you* won't be," she said, and moved to close the door.

Pierson slid his boot into the narrow opening. "Then, could I trouble you for water?"

"Well's over yonder," she said, and pushed the door; Pierson yielded. He walked to the well and lifted the dipper from the bucket. He sipped the water, taking his time, and glancing up at the cabin. The window curtain stirred and he saw Dotty peering out at him. He removed his cap again, smoothed down his curly brown hair and daringly stared up at her. They locked a momentary gaze on each other; then the curtain fell back into place.

She was in his thoughts the long week that passed. Worry chased his every waking moment. *She can't love him! She can't! She's too good for him... maybe even too good for me. But, if Dotty were mine, I'd love her and treat her like a princess. Nothing would be too good for her.*

* * * *

Pierson reported what he had seen to his commanding officer. "We don't get involved in the local business," his superior said. "Long as Mr. Beaumont minds his own business and doesn't interfere with the United States Government, he can do as he pleases," the

Captain added, "Besides, she ain't the first woman to take a beatin' from her husband, north or south."

Time was running out. The Army was on the move. John Bell Hood had shifted north, attacking the Union's precious supply line from Chattanooga. Federal General William T. Sherman was vexed that he had to expend resources to protect ground he had already covered. He ordered Gen. George Thomas and the Army of the Cumberland to move north to Tennessee. He expected Hood would attempt to re-take Chattanooga from the Union's small contingency garrisoned there. Pierson's regiment was ordered to the ready for their move north. His fear for Dotty's well-being weighed heavily on him. *I have to speak with her... convince her to leave Wilmer.*

He ventured back to the cabin one more time and knocked on the battle-scarred door. He knocked again, louder than the first.

Dotty knew Pierson was not going to leave. She walked to the door, but hesitated. "Please go," she said, tears filling her eyes. She had been faithful to Wilmer, but it made no difference to him. Regardless of where she went or what she did, she was to blame if anyone—man or woman—spoke to her. The beatings came. Any excuse would do. "You must leave, Pierson, please," she whispered, brushing at her tears. "He'll kill us both if he finds you here."

"Dotty, open the door—please," he said, and waited.

She lifted the latch, the door opened. A moment's gaze bound them in what they had both fought to accept.

"You must leave him," Pierson said, lifting her hand and placing a fold of federal greenbacks into it, then forced her hand over them. "This is all I have, they're yours... they'll get you a lot further than Confederate money."

She stared a long moment at the currency. "I can't take your money."

He lifted her chin that brought her lips so close to his. "I see you everywhere I go," he whispered.

She closed her eyes, fearing they would betray her feelings for him, a man who had invaded her country and who appointed himself her sole protector. The blush on her cheeks finally betrayed her. She stepped back into the little room; Pierson closed the door. "This is wrong," she said, turning back to him, her tears washing her blushed cheeks.

"Is it wrong to want to protect you," he asked, following her into the room.

"I know you've been watching me," she said.

"I fell in love with you."

"*He* says he loves me, too."

"Love isn't cruel, Dotty. It doesn't bruise and it doesn't break bones."

She touched his cheek and his lips covered hers with tender and gentle kisses, as loving as a kiss was meant to be. Passion overrode all reason as he pressed the full weight of his body against hers. His gentle, but hungry lips confirming all she needed to know.

"You do love me," she whispered, incredulous to the reality of what was happening to them.

"Since the first moment I laid eyes on you," he said through panting breaths. "The Army is moving us out, Dotty. I want you to go to Marietta, get a train ticket and head North...you'll be safe there. I'll find you—I swear," he said, stealing another kiss. "He'll kill you if you stay here."

* * * *

Wilmer squinted against the late afternoon sun. His head felt as though it would jar off his shoulders with each step of his plodding mare. *Ah knowed that Bastard Baldy-Bob was cutting his licker with turpentine! I'll take care of him.* He pulled up on the reins and leaned far over to one side of his horse and puked. The piney woods seemed to be swaying; it was then that Wilmer fell off the mare, which skittered a few steps away from the befouled hulk of a man. She nibbled delicately on some grass while Wilmer floundered on the red dusty road. He swiped a meaty fist across his mouth and gained his feet. "Come 'ere," he snarled and grabbed the reins. He mounted the quivering mare and continued towards home—and Dotty. *That Bitch better be in the house when I get home or I'll know why!*

The mare walked docilely into her stall; she knew better than to disobey Wilmer. Even she had not been spared Wilmer's abuse. He slopped half a pail of water into her trough, threw his saddle into a corner and sauntered out of the barn, slamming, but not latching, the door behind him.

"My God! It's Wilmer!"

Pierson calmed her with a kiss. He rested his forehead against hers for a moment, "I'll take care of him." He opened the front door and stepped out onto the porch as Wilmer reached the first step. He held his rifle at the ready, just in case. "It's over, Beaumont, you hear? No more beatings!"

Wilmer shoved the Yankee Private aside, his hand at his belt, and entered the cabin. Dotty backed away as Pierson followed Wilmer into the cabin.

Quick as a snake, Wilmer whipped the short oak club from his belt, spun around to Pierson, and struck him on the side of his head, felling the young private in one blow. Pierson's head bounced off the edge of the door frame, and his kepi fell from his hand.

Dotty caught Wilmer's arm before he struck again. "We ain't done *nothing*, Wilmer!"

He pushed her away as he bent over Pierson. "You tell me, you son-of-a-bitch, how long you been layin' with my wife?"

Pierson was out cold as blood from his head wound flowed down his ashen face.

Wilmer adjusted his grip on the club and lifted it high in the air.

Dotty jumped on Wilmer's back, her fingers clawing his face, trying to gouge out his eyes. Wilmer reached back, caught Dotty up by one arm and threw the tiny thing that she was off his back as though she were no more bother than a sparrow. "This time, I'm gonna teach you a lesson you ain't never gonna forget. Take off your blouse," he growled, kicking her legs apart as she lay sprawled on the floor. In one swift move, he tore at her blouse, his dirty nails scratching he mounds of her breasts.

Years of abuse had taught Dotty that if she struggled, the beating was worse and that Wilmer became even more aroused in the frenzy of a brutality that triggered not love or lust, but savage rape. *No! Not this time! I'd rather die than let you touch me.* She spied the old shotgun that had been propped in the corner; she didn't know whether it was loaded.

"Let your soldier boy see what he ain't never gonna sample no more," Wilmer snarled, gasping and panting as he drove his hand up Dotty's skirt, probing her soft thighs. The club lay on the floor near the struggling couple.

Tears coursed down Dotty's cheeks as Wilmer tore the buttons on his trousers, slobbering, licking, and biting Dotty's breasts.

"Get up, you filthy bastard—you sorry sack-a-shit!" Pierson shouted, cocking his rifle.

Wilmer jerked his rear in the air and pressed his hand into Dotty's chest to support himself. "The hell you say! Ain't *nobody* gonna tell me what to do in my own home!" he growled.

Pierson shoved the gun's barrel into Wilmer's back. "Get off her!"

Wilmer placated the Yank, slowly moving up off Dotty; she shoved her arm against his chest. He turned back to Pierson. "You want some of this," Wilmer said, gesturing his head towards Dotty, "I'll let you have a turn."

"Move—you pig bastard!" Pierson shouted, as his vision swam in and out of one eye; the other swollen shut.

"You ain't got the—"

The roar of the shotgun blast tore a hole in Wilmer's back from waist to shoulder, jerking and whirling him skyward before he came crashing down on the hard-planked floor

Pierson looked beyond Wilmer's blood-soaked carcass. The

force of the recoil had thrown Dotty against the wall. She stood up, dropped the shotgun, and fell into Pierson's arms, weeping the shock and relief of what she had done. "I'm not sorry. No—not one damn bit," she cried.

A week later, a curious neighbor came to the cabin. True enough, he had nothing but contempt for Wilmer, but whenever he could, he would stop by to check on Dotty. He entered the yard and saw Wilmer's horse eating grass alongside the barn. He called out, "Wilmer! Halloo the house! Miz Dotty?"

The front door was closed. It was the pungent odor of decay seeping through the loosely hung hinges that drew him to the door. He stepped inside to find a chair lying on its side next to a shotgun near Wilmer's rotting body. The look of surprise on the drunkard's face struck the neighbor as comical. He giggled and pinched his nose. "Finally, you Sumbitch. You got off easy."

The neighbor moved about and saw a Union blue kepi on the floor next to a torn and blood splattered blouse. The bedroom, he noted, was as neat as the front room was a mess. Wilmer's suit and spare shirts hung tidily on pegs. There was no sign of Dotty's clothing or any of her personal belongings. "Yeah, you bastard, you got what you deserved. Hope your Missus has some peace, whoever she's with."

* * * *

It was a winter evening in 1967. The Ball family sat in their cozy chairs in the living room watching the end of a T.V. news program before the *Wonderful World of Disney* came on. They were the latest family to reside in the old Beaumont place. Four-year-old Karen and baby John, curled up with their mother on the couch, while twelve-year-old Mary sat on the floor in front of her mother's feet. Mr. Ball sat in his brown plaid Barker-lounger.

During a commercial break, the family heard the distinct sound of someone trudging up the gravel walk, toward their front door; curiously, they had not heard a vehicle approach. Mr. Ball stood up, went to the television set and turned down the volume. "Who's there," he called out.

They heard the footsteps continue, as if through the front door, and across the living room, beyond Mary, who sat in horror, hands clapped over her mouth. Mrs. Ball clutched one-year-old John so tightly that he began to whimper in protest. Karen just looked between her parents, bewildered by the growing tension she could feel in the room.

The footsteps continued into the kitchen, then stomped across the floor. Silence emanated from the kitchen. A second pair of foot-steps clattered across the living room and entered the kitchen. Then, the whole house shook and reverberated with the heavy thud of some-thing crashing to the kitchen floor.

Mr. Ball tried to gather his wits and the courage to investigate the phenomenon, when they all heard the sound of a weeping woman coming from the kitchen. Mr. Ball could not move, even if he wanted to; and he didn't want to. The murmur of quiet conversation drifted from the kitchen. Mr. and Mrs. Ball strained to hear the words.

Now, two sets of footsteps sounded on the linoleum floor, one light, and one much heavier, moving towards the back door. They all heard the sound of the kitchen door opening and closing until, finally, complete silence descended upon the astounded family.

"What...what the hell was that," Mr. Ball said.

"Mommy, I'm scared." Mary buried her face in her mother's knees and burst into tears.

Three sets of eyes as wide as milk saucers met Mr. Ball's gaze as he slowly got up from his chair and cautiously tiptoed to the kitchen. Nothing in the room had been disturbed.

That night, the kids slept in their parent's bedroom. John lay between his parents in their maple double bed while Mary and Karen camped out on the floor in their dad's old sleeping bag. The bed-room light burned all night.

The next morning, Mr. and Mrs. Ball decided to sell the house and move closer to her parents in Sandy Springs.

The family who now occupies the home has declined all requests for interviews by this author. One can only hope that Wilmer, Dotty and Pierson have made peace with each other.

30_ Connie M. Treloar

The Swimming Lesson

*J*im and Beau were a questionable pair.

Jim was nineteen years old, the only child of a woman who had lost her spirit in the years since her husband abandoned her and their six-year-old boy. She had done everything she knew how to do to raise her son; unfortunately, sometimes *everything* is never enough. That is how it was with Jim—an unruly and sarcastic punk. Whenever a crime occurred in the river front town of Roswell, Georgia, the police always sought out and questioned Jim before anyone else.

When it was discovered that all the windows in the school buses were broken out at the end of the school term, the towns folk were quick to blame Jim. There were even accusations that Jim was the one who tortured and killed the puppy found only last week in his neighborhood.

Neighbors with a modicum of sense kept their pets away from Jim. Daughters were forbidden to talk to him—not that the girls needed the restraint; they were instinctively wary of him and the way his slow, heavy eyes strayed to their blossoming bosoms, his tongue licking his thick chapped lips, while the girls placated him with polite small talk.

His mother had reached her limit and had told a neighbor: "I wish that boy would take it into his head to move out on his own and leave me to some hard-earned peace. He's worn me out—always in trouble and denyin' he's done anything wrong."

Beau, on the other hand, was a tender soul. At twenty-five years of age, Beau was a man full grown, six foot three but, sadly, had the mind of a ten-year-old boy. He had been an easy-going infant, requiring little attention, other than feeding and diaper changing. Soon after he began putting two or three words together in a sentence, he seemed to regress. His mother made frantic trips to doctors when Beau began to babble incoherently and spent hours removing the plastic bowls she kept easy to reach in a deep drawer in the kitchen, and stacking them as high as they could go. The doctors were at a loss to diagnose the origin of his *slowness*. As the years passed, Beau continued in his simple and compliant nature, the joy of her life and reason for living. What saddened her was the cruel way in which other kids had treated Beau.

She expected the boys in the neighborhood to be mean—not cruel as they were, pushing Beau down and throwing rocks at him simply because he tried to be part of their soldier games. *"Mama, how come my friends doan like me,"* he always asked. And, the look of bewilderment in his big blue eyes tore at her mother's soul.

"They just don't know you, Beau," she would say, holding back angry tears as she applied ice to his cuts and bruises.

The girls were even more vicious and merciless. She had all she could do not to assault the little ten-year old "hussies" who pulled his hair and teased him into eating dirt clods. She even caught them daring him to pull down his pants so they could see his "weenie."

In spite of all the hate-filled and hurtful things they said and did to him, Beau never retaliated. As the years passed, the town folk actually grew to care about Beau as his mother had prayed. It didn't bother them none that he was slow – certainly not the merchants along Canton Street where Beau was a familiar sight. Dressed in his plaid shirt and jeans, with a bright white apron tied around his waist, Beau could be seen sweeping the walkways in front of the Chandlery, or lifting Mrs. Lewis' heavy-framed artwork – for the umpteenth time – until she finally decided on a suitable arrangement for the antique pieces in her collectibles shop. Yes, Beau was as much a part of the old town Square as the shopkeepers were. In the summertime, ladies would set out their tangy lemonade, welcoming him on their porches, sometimes asking him to do an odd job or two. And, during wintertime, they'd offer Beau a strong cup of coffee or hot chocolate for him to sip in their warm and inviting kitchens.

It would not be an overstatement to say that Beau's mother was far from happy about her son's friendship with Jim. She, as everyone else, knew Jim's reputation and heard the way Jim put down her son: *"Don't be so stupid... get real, you imbecile!"* She even saw Jim punch Beau in the stomach on one occasion. She confronted Jim and the pimply-faced teen said, *"Beau told me to hit him."* Her plea to Beau to limit the time he spent with Jim fell on deaf ears. *"He's my best friend, Mama,"* Beau said, with the naiveté of a child.

She couldn't control Beau's movements night and day. So, for the most part, she kept her feelings to herself, and offered up her prayers that God would continue to look after her gentle son.

* * * *

Late one Friday, Jim caught sight of Beau, walking up ahead of him, toward the town Square. The day had been perfect; there was no reason to doubt that the night wouldn't be even more perfect to camp out along the Chattahoochee River. It never mattered to Jim that it was against the law to camp out – it had never stopped him before and, as he always said: "It sure as hell ain't gonna stop me now."

Jim came up behind Beau and drove a stiff punch into his back. "I got some packages of meat and cheese and a loaf of bread," he said, then leaned closer to Beau's ear. "I lifted it from the supermarket." He snickered and popped another punch on Beau's shoulder. "I even got some beer. We'll throw out a few blankets on the river bank and make a night of it.

Beau was excited. "I'll make some peanut butter and jelly sandwiches, Jim," Beau said with a smile. "Mama doan make 'em thick the way I like," he said, but he knew the real reason: once she learned that he was going to camp out with Jim, surely she would try to discourage him. "I'll pack some potato chips and you know how I like my soda pop—real ice cold and fizzin'..." His excitement suddenly dissolved. "No, Jim. I can't go," he said, remembering his mama's words: *"I don't like you going down to the river. It's dangerous."*

"Whatsa matter—scared of your mama?"

"I doan know, Jim," Beau said, rubbing his shoulder.

"What d'ya mean you *doan know*," Jim said, mimicking Beau. "Do you wanna go or not?"

Beau looked beyond Jim; knowing he would be disappointing one or the other. Jim was his best—and only friend... mama would understand—she always did.

And, so, as the late afternoon sun began to set over the little town alongside the Chattahoochee, Beau ran to catch up with Jim. Beau slung his knapsack filled with his quickly-made peanut butter and jelly sandwiches, his bag of potato chips, and the six-pack of ice cold soda pop. They began the descent to the river's edge, to their favorite camping spot.

"When you gonna grow up, Beau," Jim growled. "Have a beer – like a *real* man. Oh... I forgot, you ain't a *real* man," Jim said, reaching into his sack and pulling out the six-pack of beer.

Beau studied on Jim for a long moment. "I am a real man, Jim," he said and rubbed his chin. "I shave, doan I?"

"That don't make you a *real* man," he said, the hiss of the pulled tab punctuating his words. "You ever have a girl?" He took a long, satisfying gulp of the brew.

Beau set his backpack on the ground. "I got lotsa girlfriends," he said.

"Them old ladies in town don't count." Jim's face was a study in anger and jealousy: *How could a moron like you be so welcomed when they wouldn't even spit on me if I was on fire?*

"They are girls, but they're my friends, too," Beau pouted through his confusion over what Jim was getting at.

"I'm talking 'bout a girl you can kiss an' do other –"

"Mama says you don't kiss a girl who isn't your wife!"

Jim laughed as he pitched the empty can into the thicket of underbrush. "Oh, that's right. I forgot." His laugh was exaggerated. "You're a *mama's boy*, not a real man."

"I told you, Jim. I am a real man... I shave."

"Shut up and hand me those blankets," he said, looking up, then down the riverbank, making sure the local police weren't patrolling.

The sun had set hours ago on what turned out to be a particularly hot July Friday. Now that nightfall had come, it seemed the heat had baked itself into the land. The toads were croaking and the cicadas chimed in, drowning out the sounds of the last commuters straggling up Roswell Road from Atlanta.

Jim and Beau made their way along the river bank of the meandering *Hooch*, as the locals called the miracle that began as a mere trickle 3,200 feet up in the Appalachian Mountain chain near Chattahoochee Gap. Jim and Beau set about making camp, ignoring the scurrying sounds about them in the woods filled with creatures— most no bigger than a good-sized raccoon, along with bears and turkeys and an assortment of other wild animals—and the old hickory, oak, and hemlock trees where Native Cherokee and Creek Indians once hunted before the white man took eminent domain.

Jim pulled a cigarette out of his shirt pocket and stuck it between his crooked teeth that clamped down on it as he spoke. "Beau, you and me gotta get us a place of our own to live. My ol' lady's a pain—always whining about pleasing the neighbors and all kindsa crap," he blew out his long puff of smoke. "I know now why my ol' man left her."

"I think your Mama is a nice lady."

"You would!" Sarcasm bit his words as he leaned over and untied his tennis shoes. He flipped the cheap acrylic blanket in the air and spread it out, moving and smoothing the folded edges with his foot. He slipped a six-inch jackknife under an edge of his blanket and quickly slapped at his neck. "Damn mosquitoes! Make it hard for a man to enjoy hisself in the woods," he said, then looked over to Beau. "Hey, did I ever tell you 'bout the slave boy who drowned – right here – right where we're lying?"

"Didn't anybody teach him how to swim?"

Jim snickered. "If you ain't the biggest idiot I ever knowed. Slaves weren't taught to swim – not back during the War Between the States, you idiot!"

"I'm sorry, Jim," Beau said with hurt. "I didn't know that."

"Jes' shut your pie hole and listen up."

"I will, Jim. I won't talk no more. Ok?"

Jim hiked his eyebrow. "Do you wanna hear about the slave, or what?"

"Yeah, Jim. I'll be quiet. Ok?"

"I was saying—back in the War, when them Yankees come here to Roswell—sumbitches burned the mill, and ran out lotsa good folk. Well, they set right here – jest before they crossed the Hooch. Them slaves weren't as loyal to the folks who took care of 'em as they shoulda been. One slave, named Joseph, offered to show the Yanks an easy way crossed the river. Somehow or nuther he got hissef kilt. Drowned. Story is, the Yanks just let him. They didn't like them slaves, even iffen they went to war over them. Took him awhile – to drown that is. So I hear." Jim snickered. "Served him right. Shoulda been more loyal to the people who looked aftah him." The beer finally hit Jim and, without another word, he just pulled the corner of the blanket up over his face to ward off the mosquitoes.

Beau inhaled the woodsy air ladened with humidity and watched the lightening bugs flitting between the branches of sweet gums. He liked sleeping under the stars—and God. "Lord, watch over mama and my friend, Jim, and those nice ladies who make me tea and chocolate. I love 'em all, Lord, and it would be nice if you remember me, too, in bad times," he whispered, then rolled to his side and heard the crunch of his bag of chips. He muttered and pulled the crushed bag from beneath his prone body.

The moon was full and riding high in the midnight sky and, despite the city lights, the stars shown brightly—almost winking, as if ready to fall asleep themselves. Traffic on Roswell Road had slowed to an occasional whisper of tires rolling over the bridge. The toads and cicadas—as if somehow controlled by a switch— ceased their moon lit concert.

Jim suddenly jerked straight up, his lip curled in poorly disguised disgust as he stared contemptuously at Beau who had fallen into a deep sleep, his head cradled on his folded arms. Jim moved into a more comfortable position on the blanket, satisfied that he still exerted control over the gentle giant of a man. "Damn fool. We could be at a club—drinkin' with the girls iffen he weren't an idiot. Damn fool," he whispered.

A ripple stirred the surface of the fog-shrouded Hooch. A fish sailed up out of the river and slapped the surface with a splash that washed against the fallen trees at the river's bank. Jim stirred, smacking his lips, while Beau slept peacefully, a thin line of drool running from the side of his mouth.

Another wider and deeper ripple appeared, its rings rushing and lapping the water's edge and then, something bobbed within the ripples – disappearing, then reappearing – as it glided closer to shore.

"Help me," was the weakened sound that hung in the heavy night air. It was a kind of whispered echo and Jim's sleep-weighted lids popped open. He felt certain that someone had murmured in his ear because the breathy sound tickled his lobe. "You say something, Beau?" A stench assaulted Jim's nose and he gagged and jumped up, hand-to-face and kicked Beau's leg. "You picked a spot with a dead animal, you idiot!"

Beau stirred. The sound of water slapping the logs lying on the bank drew Jim's attention. He turned. A tall, emaciated shape came from the fog-blanketed river. Two black holes were positioned where eyes should have been and its lips were nibbled away, exposing jagged and rotted teeth. "Help me, please help me, Massah." Heartbreak covered what was left of his face.

The form stumbled and moaned, "Help me, Massah," through a mournful cry, dragging one leg, then the other, as he closed in on Jim.

What was Jim seeing? It appeared to be a black man, hardly grown, clad only in shredded brown trousers. Its bare chest was covered with grey-green patches of sloughed off flesh that hung in tatters. The night breeze lifted the torn flesh on the arm he held out to Jim. "Joseph hept you, Massah. You gottstah help me now," Joseph said, his dangling hand coming within inches of Jim's.

"Don't touch me, boy," Jim said, stumbling backwards and tripping over a fallen pine log. The smell of rotting flesh made him retch and stress his breathing. Jim suddenly pitched forward on hands and knees, and hurled his three cans of beer, splashing his own face with the sour vomit. Jim swiped his hand across his mouth and got to his feet. The river was calm again.

"Sumbitch! Musta been that damn food," he said, walking back to his blanket, and grabbing another beer from his knapsack. "I ain't never seen nothing like that in my life," he said, guzzled down his beer, and pitched the can over his shoulder. A second later, he heaved a mighty belch, then lay back down, pulled the blanket over his face and went back to sleep.

The moon slowly moved in the night sky and, just as slowly, Joseph crawled back out of the water and seized Jim's arm, causing Jim to bolt nearly a foot off the blanket. He focused his eyes on the two hollow orbs just inches from his own. Joseph sealed Jim's mouth shut with one hand of slimy exposed bone and torn flesh. A maggot crawled from Joseph's empty eye socket and fell onto Jim's cheek, its milky-white body wriggling from the impact.

"Ah, hept you—now you gonna help me," Joseph insisted. "*Help me!*" He pulled Jim from the blanket that tangled around deadfall as Jim fought the slave.

Try as he might, Jim could not break free of Joseph's hold, or the blackberry brambles that snared his shirt, or the endless tangle of vines that tugged at his legs and feet then, he fell, face first into the river.

Beau stirred, let out a quick sharp fart and opened his eyes. In the dark, he thought he saw some movement. "Jim" he ventured. He decided not to call to his friend, again, lest he was sleeping. Beau squirmed to find some comfort on the hard ground and drifted back to sleep.

Jim furiously thrashed about, frantically fighting the water and Joseph whose voice was now filled with malevolence, his empty orbs blazing a fiery red glow. "Youse a demon whose let me drown... you ain't no good... no, suh..." Joseph's voice thundered. "Iffin the Devil won' takes yuh, Ah will!"

Jim managed to pry loose of the rotting hand as the water swallowed him again. He gasped, but only sucked in the clay-silted river. His stomach filled with cool river water. His lungs closed, sealing them against the encroachment of water and, life's sustaining air. Jim's arms floated above his head, his eyes and mouth open, as he slowly spiraled down into the murky turbulent depths. His body came to rest, snared among a deposit of garbage—bicycle tires, an old stove, and the 1955 Chevy door's hinge that snagged Jim's shirt sleeve.

A lonely, questioning hoot owl broke the deadening silence; cicadas began chirping, and croaking toads joined in their chorus.

* * * *

"No Ma'am, we don't have any new leads ...I know it's been two weeks ... Yes, I realize that Beau was the one who reported Jim missing ... No, there is no evidence of foul play — absolutely none ... We *are* treating this as a missing person's case, absolutely. We've searched the river around their camping site ... No I don't believe he drowned, especially since you indicated he could swim ... I'll keep you posted ... Yes, ma'am? ... Ok, and what's that number? ... Alright, I have it ... Yes. Goodbye."

Detective Lenny Cook spun around in his chair to face his partner. "I'd say we can put this case to rest now. If he's dead, maybe we'll get lucky and he'll show up in someone else's jurisdiction. If he's run off; so much the better. If I didn't know any better, I'd say his mother has already given up on him—she's planning an extended visit with her sister in Florida."

Soul Casualty

*U*sually, it was wide-eyed teens who came away with wild stories of a light flying through the empty brick shell that had once been a prosperous woolen mill. Young lovers and, sometimes, loners swore they had witnessed a greenish-blue human apparition streaking though what was left of the empty rooms on the ground floor of the ruins. Sometimes wisps of smoke, smelling of wet and burned wood, traveled in an unnatural manner about the building. The haunted mills were a favorite topic of conversation among the Roswell High School crowd.

Mark Hall was their star athlete. At six foot four, he made an easy target as receiver to Jason Petty's bullet-armed passes. Everyone knew Mark was a shoe-in for a free ride to UGA on a full football scholarship. Laid-back, with burred brown hair and hazel eyes, Mark was popular with the girls as well as his teammates. He was a good kid who stayed out of trouble, eschewing the use of drugs, including any kind of bodybuilding formulas. As a football player, Mark thought it was kind of sad that some people believed heavy drinking was a natural part of team sports. He drank an occasional beer at football parties because he did not want his teammates to get the impression that he thought he was better than they were.

Summer, Mark's steady girlfriend, was a serious-minded, straight-A student. When she wasn't with Mark, she enjoyed the company of one or two of her like-minded girlfriends. Mark and Summer's relationship was supposed to be on hiatus because they would be attending separate colleges and both had agreed that they could and should date other people.

They often took advantage of the solitude of the mill where, on numerous occasions, Mark and his Dad had gone exploring for artifacts. He refused to give any credence to the "ghost" stories he had grown up with and decided that if he was careful among the old ruins, nothing would happen to him or to Summer.

It was a damp and cold Friday night in October as Mark and Summer made their way through the fire-charred old ruins. The autumn moon cast a brilliant penetrating light through the missing floors, and illumined the graffiti left by explorers from other decades; *Bert & Judy 2-14-35* was crudely etched within a heart on one wall; *Peace & Love 1969* was carved in fat, balloon letters.

He took Summer's hand and guided her through the wreck, mindful of the unstable sections and rusted pipes protruding from mold stained walls. He avoided anything that awaited the slightest encouragement to collapse as he made his way to their secluded spot, sat down, and positioned his back against the dirty brick wall. He pulled a can of beer out of his coat pocket and pulled the tab. "C'mere," he said, pulling Summer down beside him. He gently tipped her chin up and kissed her. It was a long kiss that sent his tongue exploring. Summer giggled. It happened a lot when she was nervous and, despite the unfounded stories she had heard of the strange sights and sounds in the abandoned old ruins.

"Now, stop," Mark said, then burst into a laugh of his own.

"I'm sorry. I can't help it," she said, giggling her words.

"Okay, let's just go."

"No, Mark, really," she said, taking the can of beer out of his hand. "Let's stay," she said, and sipped the brew. Her face puckered with the taste as she handed the can back to him and touched his cheek with one hand, while sliding the other along his jean-clad thigh. "I want us to be together," she said, and suddenly stiffened. "I smell smoke."

"No, you don't," he said, through his kiss, his hand tangling in her long brown hair, the other exploring the small of her back.

"Suppose the building is on fire," she insisted.

"Awh, c'mon, Summer, you don't believe those ridiculous stories—"

"It smells strong in here, Mark." She backed away while peering into the darkness breached only by dashes of moonlight glancing off pools of stagnant rainwater puddled on the charred plank flooring. "Look," she whispered, pointing toward the doorway. She felt the hairs on the back of her neck tingling, and the parched feeling that seized her throat.

She and Mark stood dumbstruck watching the wisp of green-tinged smoke creeping along the floor. Summer squeezed Mark's hand as the strange substance began to take on a human form. She pounded Mark's leg, unable to say a word.

"What the hell—" he said, his eyes fixed on the glowing apparition; the beer can fell out of his hand, bubbling foam as it rolled across the floor.

The cloud-like form reacted to Mark's voice; it shot across the room and hovered near the doorway to a small antechamber. The smell of smoke intensified, though they could not see any obvious source of its choking stench. The two held each other, unable to move and feeling the intensifying urge to cough as they stared upon the apparition. It floated to a hole where a window once had been, its misty green shape taking on the spectral form of a woman wearing a 19th century day dress.

The Green Lady turned, seeming to contemplate the couple, then spun back around to the opening in the wall.

Mark tugged Summer's arm, forcing her to follow him as he crept towards the doorway that would lead them outside. At last, they were at the door. "Don't run—not yet," Mark whispered.

Just keep walking, don't panic... or you'll start running and never stop until you're in Alabama, Summer warned herself. They walked at a steady pace and then, ran the last twenty yards to his Jeep. "Hurry," she shouted and jumped into the passenger seat.

"Wait a minute..." Mark said, standing at the front bumper, fixated on the Green Lady hovering in the window, her illumination growing in intensity. The ghostly image let out a blood-curdling sound—more of agony than of threat.

Mark stumbled backwards against the hood and Summer screamed and bolted off the seat. They stared, unable to believe the ungodly image of the woman floating from window to window; a keening screech trailing behind her.

"Please! Mark, let's go," Summer screamed.

The apparition appeared in the doorway, floating, then flew at them.

Mark raced to the driver's door and jumped onto the seat.

"Start the car, damn it! Start the car!"

"I am! I am!" he said, shoving the key into the ignition.

He revved the engine, punched in the clutch and shifted into reverse. The Jeep slammed an old oak, crushing the tail light. He cursed, then threw the stick shift into first gear, and popped the clutch.

* * * *

The young couple tried to remain calm as they recounted the story to Summer's parents who gave all outward signs of disbelief. Her father turned away from his news program and cocked an eyebrow in their direction. "I don't know what you think you saw, but you two need to stay away from that old place. I'm surprised it hasn't been razed by now. By the way, what *were* you doing there?"

Their terrifying ordeal was but one more tale of the dozens that had been told of the supernatural sightings over the years. Few knew or were able to explain the origins of the ghostly apparitions that began nearly 150 years ago

* * * *

In July of 1864, Theophile Roche, the manager of the Ivy Woolen Mill, was confident he had successfully spared the mills from William T. Sherman's juggernaut. He had declared the mill a neutral entity, as evidenced by the French flag flying high over the plant. His Gallic arrogance blinded him to the realities of a war brought to his doorstep. Theophile Roche did not have long to savor his ruse.

Cavalry General Kenner Garrard arrived in Roswell to rebuild the bridge across the Chattahoochee, which had been fired by retreating Confederate soldiers. Before Garrard carried out his orders, he decided to personally inspect the wool and cotton mills. He wasn't going to be charged with negligence for leaving the enemy war-related materials. "Uncle Billy" Sherman had a blistering temper and was already incensed that his cavalry had failed to destroy all the railroad lines leading to Atlanta.

Rumors quickly flew about the spinning room, weaving their way amongst the workers who were in a dither about the arrival of Sherman's cavalry. Laney Brown tried to ignore her co-workers' nervous looks as their excited voices rose above the clatter of the machinery. Laney shifted her feet in her broken-down brogans. Though they were less than comfortable, they at least kept her feet off the hard wood floors. The constant talk around her broke her concentration; so, she decided to take a break. In a casual manner, Laney walked over to the workers' water bucket, reached the dipper, then nonchalantly slipped into the cloakroom where she knelt down, the skirt of her dress pooling in a circle about her.

A basketful of puppies whimpered and clambered over each other, vying for a choice spot near their tired mother. The beagle and cocker mix, lovingly named Blossom by Laney's co-workers, looked up with soft brown eyes. Her light brown tail thumped against the edge of the laundry basket while her four puppies struggled on their weak baby legs. "You're a good mama, Blossom, you're a good mom," Laney said, stroking the dog's head with her work-roughened hand.

"Yew best naught let Mister Stone catch yew away from your machine," Darcie Finnegan said. She was a recent immigrant from Scotland whose shining red hair was braided in a coronet about her head.

Laney tossed her head and a strand of her long black curls escaped the confines of her chignon. "And, he can jump into the river," she said, hand on hip, walking back to her place at the spinning machine.

Outside the mill, a group of cavalrymen arrived with Roche who awkwardly dismounted an army mule and joined General Garrard. Roche led the way into the mill, gesturing to one of the floor managers to shut down the machinery. "Stone, you will co-operate with the General. Show him around," the Frenchman ordered.

The bandy-legged, rotund little man eyed the General up and down, then gestured towards the gloomy workroom where Laney and Darcie were standing with their co-workers. The silence pressed their ears as the clicking and grinding machinery shut down. The workers stood, with arms crossed, glaring at the General and his contingency of soldiers who poked about the premises. The women scrutinized Garrard who nervously cleared his throat and swept his hat off his head.

The group's attention was suddenly drawn to an excited Sergeant who clomped up to the General holding a large bolt of wool cloth, locally known as "Roswell Grey." "Lookit here, General," he said, thrusting the bolt under the General's nose.

Garrard examined the cloth. The *CSA* insignia was woven into the woolen material. Garrard hiked a brow and shot a contemptuous look at Roche. "Your perfidy, I assure you, will not go unreported to General Sherman," he said, festering with contempt. "Sergeant O'Brian—arrest this arrogant French *Frog* and hold him at the town square."

"Lt. Kennedy!" Garrard snapped.

"Sir?"

"Organize a squad of men. We shall take down this building, floor by floor. Start on the fourth and set it afire. We will let the building burn down into itself. That should keep the fire from spreading to other buildings."

The Lieutenant strode off, anxious to fulfill his orders while trying to conceal his vicious delight. *These damn Rebs need to learn a lesson, the harder the better. The whole damn town should go up in flames as far as I'm concerned.* His eyes twinkled. *But, not before I get a chance to sample me some of these Rebel women...there's nothin' like a smolderin' fire in a woman.* He side-glanced the women as he climbed the stairs. *I bet these wenches haven't had a real man in a long time.*

Garrard began issuing his final orders. "Sergeant O'Brian, see that the material is removed from the building *before* it is fired. Our hospitals can use it. Distribute the rest among the women, they can have as much as they can carry."

Laney and Darcie, along with their co-workers, started toward the cloakroom to gather their dinner pails and bonnets as several Federal soldiers urged the women to hurry. After all, the Federal forces had more important things to do than deal with disgruntled women—there were card games to play, letters to write and naps to be taken. The women were propelled along and poked with Spencer rifles the soldiers laid sideways against their backs, herding them out of the building.

Approximately two hundred women stood outside the mill, loosely surrounded by dismounted cavalrymen, every fourth man holding the reins of his comrade's horse. Laney stood transfixed, a bolt of material resting in her arms, lest it get dirty in the clay dust of the mill yard. *Why do they make war on innocent women? How is destroying a mill going to help that devil Sherman? I hope he rots in Hell, if the Devil will even take the Yankee bastard!* In spite of a concerted effort, she could not hold back her tears. Darcie stood with a snarling, stony-face, one arm wrapped around Laney's waist, her own bolt of fabric dropped and forgotten in the red dust.

Lt. Kennedy appeared at the entrance of the building, followed by five hard-faced soldiers; two of whom held firebrands aloft triumphantly with monstrous smiles on their unshaven faces. Where their pockets had been empty upon entering the building, they now bulged with ill-gotten treasure. The taller of the two soldiers tossed his flaming club near the women who squealed and slapped at the glowing embers singeing their dresses.

Twenty interminable minutes passed, and then, pillars of smoke climbed high into the sky, warning neighboring communities that it was only a matter of time before they, too, would fall victim to Sherman's relentless juggernaut. The heat emanating from the fire forced the spectators several yards away and columns of smoke streamed out of the mill windows. The fourth floor, heavy with machinery, heaved a thunderous crashing sound as it collapsed onto the third floor. Cascades of ash and burning embers rained down on the spectators below. The roar of destruction drowned out the collective "Ooohhh" from the crowd.

"Let's go," Darcie yelled, taking Laney's cloth and tucking it under her arm. "No use watching our lives go up in smoke."

Laney dried her tears, rubbed soot from her heat-reddened face. Her shoulders slumped in resignation. *I'm going to starve now that the mill is gone. Mr. King will turn us out of our homes with no work to pay the rent. Where will I go? I don't even have any money to go find work. Damned evil Yankee bastards! They pity the slaves— and think nothing of destroying the lives of poor women, barely scraping by! Damn them all!*

A high-pitched bark penetrated Laney's internal tirade. *Blossom! I forgot Blossom and her pups!*

"Darcie— we forgot Blossom— she's still in there!"

"Laney, yew canna help her now. She's probably dead, her and the poor wee pups," Darcie said, refusing to let loose of Darcie's sleeve as she turned to look back at the building inferno.

"No, I can hear her! Look!"

Darcie turned around and watched as Blossom carried one of her struggling puppies in her mouth and deposited the wriggling scrap in the yard. Without hesitating, Blossom darted back into the burning building, as her puppy yipped and attempted to follow its mother.

"We can't let her burn up!" And before Darcie could answer, Laney grabbed up her long skirt and ran toward the building. At the entrance, she held an arm before her face, warding off the intense heat pouring out of the doorway. For a moment, Darcie was relieved, believing Laney had decided the risk was too great.

Laney ran into the building as Blossom came limping out again, another struggling pup in her mouth. Her tail and paws were singed; soot coated her light brown fur. She nuzzled the second pup for a brief moment, and then dashed back into the mill after Laney.

Once inside the building, Laney found it nearly impossible to get her bearings. The smoke was so thick, she could only find her way by feeling along the walls. It surprised her to be so disoriented in a place she thought she knew as well as the back of her hand. Breathing was next to impossible. When she tried, the hot air seared her lungs. A loud buzzing sound filled her ears as blackness crept across her peripheral vision; she dropped to the floor nearly blacking out. Her tortured lungs found relief in the fresher air at floor level. She rolled to her side and vomited, pulling in life-sustaining air with every heave of her failing body. Momentarily rejuvenated, she crawled as quickly as her long skirts would let her, toward the cloakroom.

Outside, Darcie begged the Sergeant to go after Laney.

"Damned, stupid woman," he cussed and ran to the entrance. A flame reached out and licked the sleeve of his wool uniform. He stumbled backwards. "No sir, no sir. That woman is done for. I ain't risking my life for no stupid Rebel woman! I'm sorry, lady."

"She's going to die!" Darcie keened, falling to her knees, clutching her arms about her. She slowly crawled toward the building, ignoring the intense heat radiating from the now fully engulfed building. Sergeant O'Brian grabbed Darcie's waist and hauled the grieving woman several yards away.

Laney crawled along the baseboard, searching for the basket. A wet nose pressed against her elbow; Blossom was back at her side. The mother watched anxiously, her eyes darting from her pups to Laney as the suffering woman scooped up the remaining pups and shoved them under her blouse. They squirmed, trying to breathe in the toxic air as their tiny pearly nails scratched Laney's chest.

Dizzy from lack of oxygen, Laney could only coax Blossom to follow along her side as she turned toward the entrance and began the long crawl back to fresh air, back to life. Her skirt caught on a large bolt in the floor. She lunged forward, trying to tear herself loose. *Don't panic, don't panic. Try to see how it's caught. Back up. Good. Ok, you've got it, now get out of here!* She edged forward, her dress pulled free. A window exploded. Glass shards cascaded and pelted her face while a six-inch slice impaled itself in her back. She bolted up on her knees, her arms flying skyward, causing her shoulder blades to pull in, driving the shard even deeper into her muscle tissue. Instinct had her thinking she could pull the shard out, but she could hardly reach it.

Blood ran down Laney's back as the jagged glass tore her flesh with every movement she made. She tried to walk on her knees, but without the use of her hands, it was impossible. With a *whoomp*, her dress ignited, the flames racing to her face. She screamed, and with the strength of desperation, stood up and began to stagger to the exit.

Blossom streaked ahead of her, half the fur on her body burned away. She howled her death throes, shot out the front entrance, and ran wildly around the crowd. Flames smoldered on her bare skin. Before anyone could come to her aid, she collapsed, shuddered and died. The grass caught fire beneath her.

A sense of satisfaction permeated Laney's oxygen-deprived brain as she saw Blossom leap through the flames and out the door.

She knew Darcie would see to the badly injured animal. All of a sudden, torturous pain consumed Laney as the flames devoured her body. She tried to strip off her burning dress and gasped when her flesh came away in pink and black strips. Horror struck. Laney screamed and screamed, racing through the flashing flames, trying to hold onto the flesh falling away from her body. Mercifully, a flaming timber crashed down, hit her head and killed her instantly.

Darcie screamed and covered her ears, trying to block out the sound of her friend's death wails, and then she fell over in a faint, clutching the two little puppies for which Laney had sacrificed her life.

* * * *

Two days later, the Ivy Woolen Mill workers were rounded up and detained by Union soldiers and held in the town square. The women stood in the hot July sun for three days contemplating their fate. The soldiers surrounded the women—there being no real means of imprisoning them—and exploited every opportunity to molest and frighten the women. A few unfortunate souls, it was rumored, were kidnapped and raped. When they were returned to the Square, their friends asked no questions.

After five long and torturous days, General Sherman ordered the Roswell mill workers to be formally charged with treason and officially placed under arrest. They were carted off to Marietta, fifteen miles away, where they were herded aboard boxcars bound for the North. The Roswell women were held under military guard until they were set free, north of the Ohio River where they could no longer engage in dangerous Rebel activities.

* * * *

In the War's aftermath, only a few Roswell women found their way back home. Darcie Finnegan, not to be bested by any damn Yankee, returned to Roswell in 1867. She found work at the newly rebuilt mill and with the money she had saved in the North, bought her own little cottage. And though no official record of Laney's death exists, the city of Roswell erected a monument near the Visitor's Center, in honor of the mill women who sacrificed so much for the Cause.

Horace...
the Horrible

52_ Connie M. Treloar

*I*t was late Spring. The dogwoods were giving up their last blossoms and the azaleas had already faded as they shied away and retreated from the growing heat of Georgia's summer sun.

I suddenly found myself braking, frantically turning my wheel to the right while, at the same time, trying to keep the car on the pavement. It was bigger than a squirrel and I did the best I could to avoid squashing it as it flew in front of my car. I felt, more than heard, the thud against the front bumper that hurled *it* about thirty feet and landed in knee-high weeds. I pulled my car off to the side of the narrow road.

Dusk was approaching, leaving the magnolias and oaks to cast their heavy shade along this section of the roadway, which made it difficult to see. I turned on the headlights before exiting the car and, in my high heels, stumbled through the weeds and grass, dreading what I would encounter.

There *it* was – I lost my breath and couldn't move.

I had seen dead animals on roadways before –who hasn't? You know how it is when you see road kill up ahead, you make a deal with yourself to turn your head so you don't see too much gore. Well, that luxury was not afforded me, the executioner.

The small, orange tabby lay there; its face mutilated beyond anything resembling a cat. I don't even think Stephen King could have adequately described what happens when a two-ton car crosses paths with a ten-pound tabby. One of his ears was torn off, showing ragged bright, blood red edges that glistened under the car's headlights. His upper lip and cheeks were smeared in a hideous grin, revealing the feline's dirt-encrusted teeth. One eye glared accusingly at me, the pupil dilated in the glare of the lights; the other eye was turned away, staring at the weeds. The tabby shuddered once, stretched out its hind legs, its one eye damning me forever. A heavy breath escaped its jutting mouth that gasped its last pull of air.

I searched the deserted lane, but there was no one. The houses along this stretch of Roswell Road were set back a couple of hundred feet and, in all probability, no one either heard or saw what had happened. The smell of chicken and warm bread wafted through the neighborhood this quiet Sunday evening. Lawnmowers and children's toys lay scattered about yards and sprinklers straddling sloping lawns *whacked, whacked, whacked* in the cool evening air.

An odd hissing sound drew my attention to the pitiful fur heap. Suddenly, the cat bolted into the air, raced across the street and up the deep lawn that formed a rise where a brick ranch stood. I started for the house, then changed my mind and walked back to my idling car, turned on the hazard lights and locked the door. I kept looking for the wretched tabby as I walked up the driveway.

"Come on up," a portly woman called from the covered porch.

"You're looking for that cat. Well, you won't find him anywhere around here," she said, stepping further out onto the porch. "My name's Natalie." She stuck out a pudgy, ring-filled hand.

"I tried to avoid hitting him... I thought I killed him!"

"You can't kill Horace," Natalie said.

"Horace?"

"He's not real."

"Not real?" *You aren't the one who hit him!*

"Come on," Natalie said, waving me up onto the porch. "Would you like a glass of tea?"

We settled into some rusted iron chairs, their paint flaking off in chunks that left patches of bare metal. Natalie's chair screeched in protest as she rocked it. "You're not from around here, are you?"

"No. I transferred here from California about a month ago. I'm still learning my way around," I said, sipping the cold, sweet tea.

Natalie settled more comfortably in her chair. "Well, it was during the war - the War Between the States - when Horace made his first appearance, about 1864... now, I know that sounds crazy, but hear me out."

She can't be serious!

You see, the Union Army occupied the town under the command of William Tecumseh Sherman," she said in her thick Southern accent. "He ordered the mill workers North, calling them "traitors." She paused and sipped her tea. "He didn't give 'em much time to get their things together; lot of 'em had pets they had to abandon. Well, they ran wild – the pets, that is. Horace was one of 'em," she said rocking and sipping her tea. "For years, folks would see him around town. Finally, it dawned on some that the cat wasn't getting any older," she said.

"You're telling me that that cat is *over one hundred forty years old?*"

"Hard to believe, ain't it? Don't take my word for it – ask around town. Go by the library. There are books about Horace – including some with pictures."

* * * *

The following Monday morning, I was at the Roswell Library's door waiting while the young girl unlocked it. I went to the reading room and paged through some local history books. The book, *"Historic Roswell in Pictures"* included a section entitled, *"We Reconstruct."* At the beginning was a photograph of the local general store, now the Public House, located on the town square. It was a grainy photo showing a man dressed in a Rebel kepi and galouses, leaning against a porch column in front of the store. His companion, a fair-haired fellow, was stooped down, petting a cat. Though the picture was a bit blurry, I could see that the cat was missing its ear. I leaned back on the chair. *You have a wry sense of humor, Natalie. You knew about this picture.*

I lifted another pictorial book and, on the second to the last page was a photograph of three young ladies in the Gibson style, mutton chop sleeves, wearing large picture hats. They were standing on the front steps of the Presbyterian Church on Mimosa Street. Half-hidden by one of the columns was the silhouette of a cat – yes a cat – and as I looked closer, I saw that it had an ear missing, or perhaps folded down. Gibson dresses were popular in the 1890s – and Natalie said that the cat had been abandoned at the end of the war – around 1864. *That's a thirty-year span of time! No way! Cats don't live thirty years!*

I went to the woman at the information desk. "Have you ever heard of Horace? The cat that's missing an ear and is *supposed* to have been a stray because it was left behind during the Civil War?"

"Are you looking for information about Horace," she asked.

"So you have heard of him."

"I've lived in Roswell my whole life," the librarian said. "Horace is part of our local lore – if you believe in that sort of thing. I have a microfiche copy of our paper with the last article written about him, if you'd like to read it."

I kept advancing the microfiche film until I found the article, *HORACE THE HORRIBLE STILL IN RESIDENCY*. It was dated October 31, 1979, and under the headline, the following:

> Those who knew and loved Horace can take comfort in the fact that he is still alive and well in our fair city. Last seen in front of Bulloch Hall on Tuesday, our famous feline threw a scare into an Alabama tourist, causing her to clip one of our 100-year-old oak trees along Bulloch Street with her car.
>
> "I tried to avoid hitting a cat," the shaken woman explained, tightly clutching her pocketbook. "But I know for a fact that I did hit him. When I looked to see where he went, a horribly injured animal ran away from me."
>
> When this reporter informed her that she had in fact hit a "phantom" cat, the woman reacted with disbelief. "It weren't no phantom. I felt my car hit that animal. I still don't see how it could have run away, it was so banged up."
>
> Horace has been putting in appearances in Roswell since 1864. It is believed he was left behind when mill workers were arrested and sent north during the Northern occupation of Roswell. As there were many other dogs and cats abandoned, the story is that Horace was attacked by a pack of stray dogs, mangling him horribly. The feline

made his first known home in 1865, with Mr. Homer Spence, owner of the Roswell General Store. He took in the orange tabby that was missing an ear and had deep gashes in his face. Spence named the cat "Jefferson" after Jefferson Davis, President of the Confederate States of America. Residents recalled the tabby that, for several years, had slept on the front porch of the general store. When the cat died in 1880, Mr. Spence buried him at the foot of his family plot in the old Woodstock Cemetery, and installed a monument of a one-eared cat, in Jefferson's honor.

Two years later, a cat, resembling Jefferson, also missing an ear, made his home with the rector of the first Presbyterian Church on Mimosa Blvd. Congregates fondly recalled the cat that occasionally sat in on sermons in the church that was used as a Union hospital during the War.

Sometime after 1900, the cat made his home with the Wing family of Bulloch Hall. In 1905, President Teddy Roosevelt paid his respects to the Wings who then occupied his mother's childhood home. The President remarked that the story of the tabby was a "Bully" one and that his mother, Mittie Bulloch Roosevelt, would have enjoyed the tale.

Then, about 1918, after paying his respects to a son who died in World War I, Roswell resident Mr. Earl Conklin was followed home from Woodstock Cemetery by – you guessed it – a one-eared orange tabby. Mr. Conklin named the cat "Horace," in honor of his dead son. The grieving father and tabby were observed together for many years thereafter in the vicinity of the old man's house on Norcross Street. "Horse apples!" was Mr. Conklin's reply when his neighbors told him that his new feline friend was at least fifty-five years old.

Apples or not, residents still believe to this day that the one-eared cat seen around town is, indeed, Horace. Not his ghost; not a cat that looks like him – but a bona fide "UN-Reconstructed" cat from the War Between the States.

I went back to the librarian once more and asked where I might find Horace's "final" resting place. She gave me directions to the Woodstock Cemetery, just beyond the fire station, on Alpharetta Street. I located the Spence family plot and, there it was, the monument to Horace. The statue was only twelve inches tall and badly worn with age. And though the statuette was roughly cut, there was no mistaking the fact that the ear had never been carved into the original stone sculpture.

I thought about that newspaper story as I drove home. I waved to my neighbors who were walking their dogs, and they waved back. I found the people who had been raised in the South were very friendly and so very well mannered. Life was certainly a lot slower here than in California. I did, on occasion, find that Southerners could be a peculiar lot – not only do they live in the past, the past lives with them. To be perfectly honest, I was pleased to find that my adopted town had such a colorful history. I pulled into my drive, turned off the ignition, and sat admiring my new home and the yard with its magnolia tree and the crepe myrtles lazily swaying in the breeze.

"Horse apples," I laughed as I got out of the car. *Haven't heard that one in a while!* I picked the newspaper off the front walkway and waved to my neighbor who was watching her three-year-old watering their concrete driveway, the water running in a stream that became a gurgling brook at the curb.

"Hey you," she called out to me.

"How's it goin'? How is Becky's skinned knee?"

"She's fine, after going through 'bout ten band-aids. By the way, did you get a new cat," she asked.

"Cat?"

"Well...a cat has been sitting on your back steps most of the day. Thought maybe you picked one up at the shelter, 'cause it sure is an ugly thing. Becky thinks it's deaf since it's missing an ear..."

I felt the blood drain from my head as I stumbled through the grass to the back of the house, clutching my newspaper to my chest, my purse banging my thigh.

"Kitty? Here, kitty, kitty... Horace?"

58_ Connie M. Treloar

Jack's Oath

*T*he worst nights, the wind carried a howling that ended in a keening wail. Deadfall, tangled in the lichen-studded oaks, trembled with the slightest breeze. Nocturnal animals scurried about their business, oblivious to the horrific scene that played repeatedly through the years since an innocent man had been murdered; his crime: the desire to move on from the horrors of war. On occasion, an especially brave individual would enter the woods next to Vickery Creek, challenging the inky dark and supposed phantoms that haunted the area just below Founder's Cemetery. The truly brave (or very drunk) made the pilgrimage on the night it was supposed to have happened; August 31st.

* * * *

Jack Smith, a quiet bachelor of twenty-eight years, lived on the outskirts of Roswell. Men respected him. He had a reputation for being an honest, hard worker. If a man needed a favor, he knew he could count on Jack. The young Floridian, a veteran of the last Seminole War, arrived in Roswell in 1857, shortly before the Seminoles were subjugated. He had survived a head injury and attempted scalping. The army doctor had performed a trephine operation; that of lifting the sections of his depressed and fractured skull with surgical instruments to relieve the pressure on his exposed brain. Jack lay in hospital for three months while his shattered skull knitted back together. All he had left to remind him of his war service were scars under his hairline and memories that sometimes left him gasping and sweating in the middle of his repeated nightmares.

Jack's bachelor status was an opportunity for Roswell's fairer sex to improve their lot in life. The women who worked in the factory naturally flocked to his side; he was an attractive man, blue-eyed with blonde hair and a close beard kept neat by the town's Negro barber. His eye-catching visage aside, the women sought his companionship because he was self-employed, owning wagons and teams and hiring himself out to the Roswell Manufacturing Company when it suited him. With Jack, a lucky girl could elevate her social and economic standing in town. For, unless you were born into one of the founding families, or "Colony," as they were collectively known, you could count on a hard life with little opportunity to advance your station in life.

Jack was polite to the women, tipping his hat in passing, and sometimes attending their socials. However, they ambushed him at church, under the guise of discussing the "Good Book." Yet, he was far from the point of settling on any special woman. That would come later, once he had saved enough money to set up a proper household and support a family.

Jack's drayman contract with the area's various mills kept him out of the Confederate Army. The mills that manufactured tents, ropes and cloth for the Confederacy, were a necessity for the war effort. Although Jack was a loyal Southerner, he had seen a lifetime of violence and death during the Seminole Wars. He knew there was nothing gallant about taking a man's life or ennobling to see a man trip over his own glistening entrails while he tried to carry a wounded comrade away from the carnage of battle. No, Sir! He'd seen enough butchery to last a lifetime!

For months, Jack had been expecting Mr. King to shut down the mills. Federal General William T. Sherman was marching south through Georgia at the rate of a mile a day since his departure from Chattanooga, in May. Eventually, word had spread that the mills would operate until the enemy shut them down. As late as the morning the mills were destroyed by fire, cloth and yarn from the factories had been delivered to cotton factors in Savannah.

In July, 1864, Federal Cavalry General Kenner Garrard was in charge of building a bridge across the Chattahoochee River. His contingent, consisting of twenty-five hundred men, occupied Roswell after putting down riots perpetrated by the town's rabble. An uneasy relationship was established between the invading army and the townspeople. The Yankee soldiers behaved, for the most part, and the town riff-raff kept a lower profile while the invading army was present. Eventually, Sherman deployed his cavalry to the south and west of Roswell in order to isolate Atlanta from her critical supply lines. General Garrard left behind a small garrison of soldiers to "keep the peace."

Jack was a practical man. He was frustrated by war shortages and the inability to conduct business and life in a normal manner. He had never owned any slaves; in fact, when he had the funds before the war, he had employed two free black men as teamsters. He was sick to death of funerals and wraith-like widows silently drifting like shadows through town, discretely asking for a handout; though they would rather have died than acknowledge that was what they were doing. Men wrecked by Shiloh, Gettysburg and Chickamauga, shuffled through town; broken in body and spirit. Some veterans already sat on the porch in front of Homer Spence's general store and made plans for "when the war is over..."

Like most citizens of the town, Jack knew that with the fall of Atlanta, the war was near over and he was brave enough to say so publicly. He knew the Yankees would dictate the affairs of the South for years after battle-weary Confederates returned home to hungry families and unemployment. He decided his best course of action was to take their damned oath of allegiance to the United States Government, and get on with making a living in the newly-united country where "where might makes right."

* * * *

One blazing hot day, Jack approached the young union soldier who usually could be found hanging around the general store. He nodded to Homer, who was organizing sparsely-stocked shelves. Private Robison, a mournful-looking fellow, was quick to respond to any affable approach made by a local resident. Fragments of peanuts flew from his mouth when he stood at attention upon being addressed by Jack. "Sir?"

"Who do I need to talk to about taking your blasted oath of allegiance," Jack asked.

Homer swallowed part of his tobacco quid and coughed.

"If you ask for Lieutenant Kennedy at Barrington Hall, I'm sure he can accommodate you, Sir," Private Robison said. "I'd be happy to escort you there, myself."

"Don't bother. Word'll get around soon enough that I've gone traitor."

Homer came from around the counter. "Are you sure 'bout this, Jack?"

"I'm not sure of anything, these days, Homer."

* * * *

Buckley Stone *was* sure of one thing; he did not appreciate anyone who made an honest living. His family, including his brother, Josiah, took a dim view of him and distanced themselves from the troubled, rabble-rouser he was. Josiah Stone, one of the mill foremen, failed in his attempt to get Buckley a job at the mill; such was his reputation. Too lazy to seek work on his own – and too untrustworthy to be hired by anyone with the sense of a flea – Buckley lived parasitically on the fringes of town, operating the odd poker game with Baldy-Bob or running liquor for the old man when his rheumatism flared up.

His circle of acquaintances included army deserters and convicted felons; ruthless men, with slatternly mistresses who made their living by stealing, gambling or, in some cases, murder. Loosely known as the "Roswell Ruffians," they had a well-deserved reputation for crime and violence. Privately, many of the law-abiding citizens hoped the Federal soldiers would stay indefinitely. The *Ruffians* kept a lower profile since the occupation, and the residents were grateful; though they would be damned if they said so!

Jack did his best to avoid the *Ruffians*. Buckley Stone was their front man and Jack had already angered the maladjusted misfit. Buckley repeatedly demanded that Jack hire him as a teamster, and Jack parried the volatile man's attempts to bully him into a job. The proximity of their hovels to Jack's cabin forced him to greet the cretins.

Sometimes, Jack would set a plate of molasses cookies out on his stoop for the hungry-looking *Ruffian* offspring; a gift from one of the women hoping to entice him into matrimony with her baking. The children were half-wild from lack of food and attention – except for slaps from their worn-out mothers – and scurried away from the cabin when he tried to talk to them. Tommy was the exception. The tow-headed, nine-year-old boy, oldest of a passel of six children, sometimes slipped into Jack's shed and currycombed his horse.

It was common for Tommy to shadow Jack's movements about town and, on at least one occasion, Jack caught the boy looking into his cabin window as he read the newspaper beside a warm fire.

Jack was asleep late one Saturday night in August, when four men burst into his bedroom. They shoved a strip of dusty burlap into his mouth, dragged him across the heart pine floor, and pounded him senseless while shouting,"Yankee lover... coward... traitor!" Jack struggled to stay conscious. His arms were jerked up behind his back, and tied with another length of burlap.

He was lying across the back of his horse when he regained his senses and saw the mill hands' simple dwellings. The moon had gone down for the night. The narrow streets were deserted and decent folks were asleep in their beds.

A cold and clammy sweat poured down Jack's face and crept from under his armpits. His mind raced frantically to think of a way to escape. The smell of scorched wood and the gurgle of the creek alerted him that he was near the cotton mill at Vickery Creek–one of the many mills the Yankees had burned the previous month.

The group halted Jack's horse beneath a large oak. One of his four captors threw a rope over a stout limb. To Jack's shame, he lost his urine that saturated his cotton drawers and dribbled down his leg. His hands worked at the burlap that bound his wrists together.

The men drew a noose about Jack's neck, and threw the other end over stout limb. The men stood looking at their leader. He finally spoke. "Give him a minute to say his last." He tugged the wad of burlap out of Jack's bleeding mouth.

Jack spit out a gob of blood and snot. "That you, Buckley? You won't get away with this. You cut me loose, I swear, I won't say anything."

Buckley spat between his booted feet and turned to his companions with a maniacal grin on his swarthy face. "I don't 'spect he's got anything to say after all. Hang him."

The men hauled on the rope. Jack's feet scrabbled in the air, two feet above the forest floor. His secured hands finally came loose and he seized the noose about his neck, desperate to get a finger under the rope for one, small, precious breath of air. His flailing body danced at the end of the rope as a macabre puppet controlled by brutal men who had forestalled the inevitable.

His tongue began to turn blue from lack of oxygen, and then, it began to protrude from his bruised, cut lips. They eased up on the rope; just enough so the balls of his feet supported his sagging weight. His bowels let go and the disgusted men hoisted him up in the air once more. He emitted gurgling sounds after he managed to slip a finger under the noose.

Buckley tied the end of the rope to the oak. He hooted in derisive laughter. "Look at 'im dance! Those women in town won't find him so purty, now!" He turned from the dying man and grabbed the halter of Jack's horse.

The four men made their way back up the path, passing a bottle of corn liquor amongst them – congratulating each other on a job "well done." Buckley suddenly stopped walking. "Quiet! I hear something." He moved to the side of the path and parted a large tea olive bush. "Boys, lookit here!" He bent down, almost to the ground, peered into the bush, and snarled, "Too bad you was such a nosy bastard."

* * * *

They were almost to Founder's Cemetery when Brett, a high school senior, realized where Mike was driving him. "I know you don't like to fool around with this stuff," Mike said, "but I thought, seeing how you're moving to Florida soon, you'd be a Bud, and tell me if you think anything really happened here after the Yankees took over Roswell," Mike said. "You know, about the guy who was supposedly hung for taking the oath of allegiance to the Federal government?"

Mike was referring to Brett's psychic ability or "Tuit" as his Gram had always called it. *Why, son, it just runs in the family. Your PaPa had it. And, now you do, too.*

He was almost seven years old before he realized he was different. Sometimes, he could see people in funny old costumes. He learned not to say much about it. His dad understood, though. His Dad was the only one he could talk to when his *Tuit* got too scary.

Besides seeing apparitions, Brett had the uncanny ability to anticipate an event before it happened. In the summer of 2001, he dreamed repeatedly that a plane had run into a giant apple. It made no sense, even to a ten-year-old, and he would have dismissed it as a silly dream, but every morning when he awoke, he was stricken with body-paralyzing sadness. September 11th dawned, blessedly dream free for the boy, only to evolve into a national nightmare.

"We'll just poke around. If we don't see anything, we'll leave," Mike said.

The boys hiked down the lane to the edge of Vickery Creek. The switchback road they took had been built by slave labor in the 1840's. Stacked-stone re-enforcing walls towered ten feet above their heads as they moved down the muddy lane, talking about their college plans. Brett was going to attend Florida State and Mike was planning on a Bulldog legacy.

"I'm going over there," Mike said, pointing to the east side of the mist-shrouded creek. "I can cross here, where it's shallow. Holler if you see or hear anything!"

Brett sat on a fallen log and picked up a stick. He drew circles in the sand and adjusted his butt on the hard, curved surface. The creek water flowed quickly, gurgling past eddies and debris washed from further up the creek. Overhead, an owl hooted. Brett tipped his head back and strained in the darkness to see the raptor.

"Shrrrrrrkkkkk!"

"Jesus H. Christ! What the hell is that?" Brett shouted to the woods about him. It was a rhetorical question, because, to be perfectly honest, he was hoping no one—and nothing—would answer him.

A squirrel, its bushy tail twirling, was suddenly snatched from the log beside Brett. A barn owl swooped down, seized its prey, and flew off with its struggling and shrieking, midnight snack. Brett jumped up and tried to determine the direction in which the owl flew. He saw Mike sloshing across the creek toward him.

"Was that you screaming like a Girlie-girl," Mike asked.

Brett landed a quick punch on Mike's shoulder. "You'd scream too, if an owl grabbed a squirrel 'bout two feet from where you were sitting. Let's go. I'm hungry. My mom went grocery shopping tonight."

"I love it when my mom goes grocery shopping!" Mike rolled his eyes. "So, I take it, you didn't see anything... did you get any weird feelings?"

"I told you before, Mike, I don't have control over my *Tuit*," Brett said. "The older I get, the less often I get feelings or see something." Brett stumbled along the path and a white spherical object rolled from under his feet.

Before Brett could bend down to examine the object, a low humming began in his ears. He intuitively turned around and looked back down to the creek beneath the switchback road.

The mist hanging over the creek had spilled onto the banks along the shoreline. Brett's gaze was fixed as he watched the scene of five men and a horse, swaying in and out of a white cloud and forming a rough, black-and-white tableau. He jerked his head and the humming became words, "*Won't get away... cut me loose...*"

"What the fuck," Mike said.

Brett grabbed Mike's sleeve. "You see them, too?"

"I take back everything I ever said about your Tuit."

"Can you hear what they're saying," Brett asked.

"They're *talking*?"

Brett repeated the words he was hearing: "I won't tell... please let me go, Buckley..." Brett fell silent. "My God," he said, "They're going to hang a man!"

"We have to do something!"

"It's not real, Mike," Brett said, taking a step backwards, then stumbled over a white, grinning skull. Something about the sightless orbs beckoned him to pick up the head. As his fingers grasped the pitiful, fractured cranium, a pain shot through his body – a bizarre and frightening feeling Brett had never experienced before. It was as though a sledgehammer smashed the top of his head, driving pieces of bone down into his spinal column, the rush causing a back-breaking agony that shot through his whole being. Brett dropped to his knees.

Mike continued staring at the group of phantom lynchmen – until one of them looked in the direction of the two boys. The apparition lifted his arm and pointed menacingly toward the teens, then distanced himself from the other ghostly images, moving directly for the two boys.

Tears flowed down Brett's cheeks.. His tears freaked out Mike, but not nearly as much as the specter approaching them. Brett's eyes rolled back in his head; he was no longer conscious of Mike or anything in the moment. A strange transformation had begun.

Brett was now a very young, and very terrified boy.

"You killed Jack," the young boy sobbed, trying to twist free from Buckley as he planted an ineffectual punch into the man's gut. I'm telling the soldiers – they'll get you! Jack was my friend!"

"You ain't gonna tell anyone anything, you snot-nosed whelp," Buckley said, shoving the outraged child to the ground, then picked up a rock, about the size of his fist, and held it high over the child's head. *Brett cowered, his shoulders rising up to the level of his ears as he anticipated Buckley's blow.*

Buckley's first strike missed Tommy's head and glanced off his bony shoulder, breaking the jutting collarbone. *Brett screamed and looked up.*

Tommy locked eyes with the man who was possessed of pure evil. He opened his mouth...

A scream – no! – a wailing, unlike anything Mike had ever heard, assaulted his senses. His gaze dropped to his friend whose kind and gentle countenance had changed into that of the terrified little boy.

There could be no other explanation: Brett was possessed as a wailing lament raced from Brett's mouth. It was not of this world – it couldn't be. Its sound was the wail of sorrow and rage wrapped in all the injustice, pain and fear every man, woman and child who walked this earth had ever suffered.

Silence suddenly felled Brett. His screaming howl had miraculously released him from whatever possessed him. He shook his head, an action that triggered his senses. He slowly got to his feet, still cradling the fractured skull against his body.

Mike, his reluctant witness to the supernatural event, stood with knees knocking so hard that he thought they would shatter. He stole a quick glance to the creek where the phantoms stood. They were gone and so, too, the graven haze that had settled over the banks of Vickery Creek.

* * * *

A forensic anthropologist confirmed that the skull, along with a fractured collarbone and broken finger bones, belonged to a child; likely no older than eight years old. Without the pelvis, there was no sex determination. The bones were at least a hundred years old, but more than that, all she would say was that the poor innocent was a homicide victim.

In deference to the insistent young man who had discovered the bones, the doctor named the child, *Tommy*...

Unforgettable

70_ Connie M. Treloar

Grief weighted her, as if a stifling, black cloak hung upon her shoulders. The velvet, blood-red lining of the mantle nurtured her. There were days she welcomed the comforting drape as a shield against the unfathomable reality of her new station in life. Other times, she found the folds cumbersome, impeding the evolution of who she was becoming.

At twenty-two, Julie Hughes could have been a college student looking forward to a full and exciting life, not living a sorrow-filled existence as a young widow. With a death grip, Julie clutched the few precious memories of the two years she had shared with her handsome, young husband, Stephen, who was a war hero. The posthumous honors bestowed upon him, however, were a cold comfort to her, and the shuttling from distant relatives to friends, in an effort to assuage her grief, did little, but serve to deepen the emptiness that consumed her.

Six months later, Julie returned to her efficiency apartment near Marietta Highway, in Roswell, exhausted in mind and body and even more depressed despite the attentions of well-meaning loved ones. It was a reprieve to be home amongst the familiar keepsakes in the apartment she had rented soon after Stephen volunteered for duty in Vietnam. Memories of him were lovingly tucked into a shoe box containing his few letters and the photographs of him and his brother soldiers, some of which were taken during R-and-R as he and his comrades wandered through Saigon. Their exuberant smiles belied the strain of training South Vietnamese soldiers in warfare during the last three months of Stephen's life. Other photos were taken in the suffocatingly green South Vietnamese jungle overrun with dangling, intertwined vines seeming as vipers snaring the young intruders.

The photo that haunted Julie the most was of Stephen alone; the rangy six-foot length of him sitting crossed legged on his cot writing his last letter to her through shafts of light, overshadowed with stripes of darkness, obscuring the man marked by time. His regulation crew cut had grown out and his young face looked tired and unshaven. His O.D. green T-shirt, hung over loose-fitting kaki shorts, and his dog tags glinted in the strange shock of light that caught it. His face was a study of wistful longing, conveying more to her than the four-page letter he was writing. She remembered reading his words of discouragement over how little an effect his training was going to have over the volunteer army: *"The men are ill-equipped. They are farmers, mostly, who are used to wielding rakes and hoes, not M16s. But, I see their determination to protect their families and land from the Communist Chinese and the Vietcong. The French made a mess here and pulled out... now, we've been given the job of trying to clean it up..."*

When Julie felt very brave, she would pull the box from her lingerie drawer, and indulge her memories of him that, inevitably, gave way to anger and emptiness. *It was just supposed to be a training mission. What went wrong? I needed you so much more than they did.*

It was June 1963, when she decided to find a job, even though a modest family trust and a hefty insurance policy provided financial security. She felt her spirit fading in the tomb of her small apartment that served as her temporary retreat from the world. It was time to move on, though she feared the unknown that lay ahead of her. And so, despite her hesitations, she showered, put on some make-up, and arranged her hair in a French twist, confirming her decision to re-enter the world. She stepped into a lemon-yellow sheath, eschewing stockings and girdle in deference to the heat, and then slid her size five feet into white patent leather sandals.

She poured herself a cup of black coffee and sat at the shiny chrome kitchen table, and nibbled at a slice of dry toast. Her eyes drifted to the headline in the morning paper; it was dismal: MEDGAR EVERS ASSASSINATED. She sighed and turned to the classified ads at the back of the newspaper. A small item in the lower right corner caught her eye, *Smith Plantation Needs Volunteers.*

* * * *

"You're all hair and eyes... just hair and eyes, my dear," Earladene Farthington said, smiling and grabbing a hold of Julie's hand and pulling her across the threshold into the hall of Smith Plantation. "When you called to say you wanted to volunteer, I couldn't get into my girdle fast enough!" Then, Earladene leaned into Julie's ear and whispered, "I take it off every chance I get – but, don't tell anyone. The busy bodies in town would have a field day," she said, pausing for a breath. "Can you imagine!" Earladene brayed with a shoulder-shaking laugh.

The matronly docent wasted no time ushering Julie through the plantation, firing off facts about the house, and offering unsolicited, though kind, advice and guiding Julie to the small kitchen. "This used to be the Warming Kitchen during slave times. It was renovated in the 1940's when the plumbing was installed. Isn't it cozy?" she asked.

It was cheery with the summer sun glancing off white painted metal cabinets and the tin canisters that lined the counter. A Corning Ware coffeepot sat in the large one-piece porcelain sink. The enamel-topped stove and refrigerator were almost brand new.

"You need to put on some weight, or you'll just blow away!" Earladene stuck a Wedgwood plate full of chocolate chip cookies under Julie's nose and continued clucking, like a mother hen. "Here, have a cookie. No, have two! I made them myself," she said, and scooped up one for herself. "The house was built in 1845... three generations of the Smith family have lived here."

Julie nibbled her cookie as Earladene continued.

"We've been very lucky here. Everything you see in the house belonged to the Smiths," Earladene said, taking another quick bite of her cookie. "It's all here," she said handing Julie a notebook entitled *Docent Handbook*. "Now, don't think you have to memorize it all at once."

Julie casually paged through the book.

"I hear someone at the door. Guess I'm on!" Earladene waddled to the kitchen door, her backside shifting from side to side, like a wigwagging railroad signal. "You just set and read. And, eat..."

Julie turned pages, and found a section devoted to photographs taken of the family. Stern faced men and humorless-looking women stared back at her. She turned another page and pulled a breath.

She didn't know why, but the image of a young Confederate officer captivated her. "Major Samuel McIntosh Lightfall, CSA (1835-1863), husband of Caroline Barnwell Lightfall," she said, reading the notation below his picture. Samuel gazed at her with light eyes set deep into a handsome face. A modest mustache accentuated his aquiline nose and the cleft in his square jaw. He had the barest hint of a smile and his eyes crinkled at the corners with humor; it was an unusual facial expression for a 19th century daguerreotype. The high collar of his uniform was partially obscured by locks of his blonde hair. *He was only twenty-eight years old,* she thought, and slowly turned the page.

"Caroline Barnwell Lightfall (1841-1863)," she said staring at the picture of Caroline who looked calmly from the page, her dark black hair sharply parted in the middle. The large garibaldi sleeves of her flower-sprigged gown dwarfed the tiny-looking woman. Caroline Barnwell Lightfall was cousin to the second generation of Smiths, as the genealogy stated.

Julie flipped the page back to Samuel's picture. It appeared to be almost contemporary – as though he had donned a costume and had his picture taken as recently as yesterday. *He was so young when he died. Just like Stephen.* She turned back to Caroline's photo and noted the year of her death – 1863. *She probably died of a broken heart.* She sighed, and caught the tear at the corner of her eye.

Over the next few days, Julie read the *Docent Handbook*, acquainting herself with the history of the Smith family. Archibald and Anne Smith had the home constructed. During the Civil War, Archibald offered haven to his niece, Caroline, while her husband fought bravely with Cobb's Legion. The young Major Lightfall died in the battle of Chickamauga on September 19, 1863, and Caroline perished a month later, while giving birth to a stillborn son.

"Do you have the original photo of Samuel in the house?" Julie asked Earladene who sat next to her, reading a fashion magazine.

"Why, yes we do." She licked the tip of her finger and turned the page. "It's on the bureau in the upstairs hall. I'm surprised you haven't noticed it," she said, leaning close to Julie and whispering, "I've seen you mooning over his picture in the Handbook." Earladene winked with a smile. "You scoot on up there. Wait! Now that I think about it – maybe I can get my hands on the letters Caroline wrote to him. I believe they're still on the premises. Even an old nanny goat like me gets a romantic thrill over them." She batted her eyes with great exaggeration and fanned herself. "I always thought they should have been published."

Julie climbed the narrow stairwell to the second floor. On the landing, to her right, a cobalt-blue lamp rested on a three-drawer bureau; next to the lamp stood a small copper daguerreotype. She picked it up, and gazed into Samuel's face. *Oh, this is so much nicer than the copy in my book! I wish I had known you, Major Lightfall. And to think, you must have held this in your hands before you gave it to Caroline...*

She touched the glass protecting the picture and before she realized what she was doing, the picture was at her cheek, warming the glass that separated her from Samuel. *What am I doing? Oh, Stephen, it's you I miss...with all my heart. I still can't accept that I will never see you again.*

"Here they are," Earladene panted, stepping onto the landing at the top of the stairs.

With flushed embarrassment, Julie put the photograph back on the bureau and quickly turned to the large Audubon prints that lined the upstairs hallway.

Earladene walked over to the photo of Samuel and picked it up. "Such a handsome devil. The South lost so many men, just like him," she said, shaking her head. "Such a tragedy. Well, it was a blessing that he never knew his wife and child had died." She shook her head, again.

Julie felt the pain of Earladene's words. "You say you have letters written by Caroline?"

"Right here," Earladene said, handing her the box of letters. "We display these 'bout once a year when we do our Civil War exhibit. You're welcome to read them, but you can't take them home – I'm sure you understand."

"Of course," Julie said, eagerly reaching for the box. "How is it that we have Caroline's letters to Samuel, but not his to her?"

"After Samuel was killed, his aides-de-camp gathered his effects and sent them to Caroline," again Earladene shook her head. "Poor thing. It must have killed her... uh... I mean, it... it must have been very hard to receive his personal belongings after he passed." She stared a long moment at Julie, then reverently placed Sam's photo back on the bureau.

"I have a photo of my husband taken the day before he died," Julie said, feeling a thickness in her throat and then, glanced a delicate swipe against the tip of her nose. "Somehow, it seems so terribly unfair that these incidental things survived and he didn't," she said, turning as tears streamed down her cheeks.

* * * *

Earladene's latest gastric delight, Apple Pandowdy, went uneaten. She silently picked up the plate, placed the dessert in foil, and rinsed the plate in the sink in the kitchen. Julie sat at the table and placed the book of letters on the table. Earladene reached out to pat Julie's hand, but thought better of it. She turned and left Julie alone with Caroline's letters.

July 15, 1862

Dear Samuel,

I volunteer to knit socks for the soldiers and pick lint for bandages. These tasks keep my mind occupied. Every time I roll a new bandage, I pray that you will not be the one to use it. I know that is wicked and selfish of me, but these words are for your eyes only!

Aunt Anne and Uncle Archibald are very kind to me. Cousins Lizzie and Helen do their best to keep my spirits up. I know they are as worried about Cousin Willie as I am about you.

Oh, my love, are you comfortable? Tell me about your accommodations. Have you sufficient supplies? We all pray that the Yankees will realize it is futile to hold us in a union we no longer desire.

Samuel, you have been gone but a few weeks and yet it seems eons. My health continues to be good, though I was feverish and a little bilious last week. Our little treasure is secure. The girls here all bid me to take care not to overtax myself.

All my Love,
Caroline

* * * *

Julie fell in love with the old plantation home, but her thirst for information about Samuel and Caroline was insatiable. She read and re-read Caroline's letters. Her preoccupation with the house and its former occupants distracted her from the pain of Stephen's loss for hours at a time. She wandered through the rooms, adjusting a picture here, patting a needlepoint pillow there, as though she were the mistress of the house, rather than one of its historical guides.

The pianoforte seemed to beckon her to the parlour and, once there, she would plunk a key or two, wishing she could play. She imagined the ladies of the home patting their chignons as they stood before the gold gilded mirror just prior to greeting a caller, and then she pictured herself, gathered with the family around a kerosene lamp in the parlour, to sing, knit or just plain gossip. The images were clear enough as she gazed into the mirror of imaginary fantasies.

Earladene sat reading Caroline's letters late one afternoon, while Julie sewed at the kitchen table. "It's a disappointing shame we never found any of Samuel's letters. I just know Caroline had to have saved them," Earladene said.

Julie bit the end of the black thread she was using to hem her antebellum-styled dress. "Maybe she hid them because they were too personal to be read by any one else," she said, and continued constructing the dress of black broadcloth that would lie over the large hoop and yards of petticoats. She even found an antique mourning bonnet with a long, crepe veil attached. Some of the other docents wore brightly colored hoop skirts, but no one wore widow's weeds.

"You know, Julie, you don't have to wear that depressing black dress. I think you're too young and pretty to be costumed like that."

"I'm a widow, Earladene. I'll wear weeds if I want to," Julie said, standing and holding the gown up to her.

Earladene pouted and tucked a strand of bleached-blonde hair back into her beehive hairdo. "You may be a widow, Miss Julie, but you don't have to look like a ghost fixin' to pop out of a closet!"

"That's a great idea," Julie laughed and leaned over to hug her indignant friend. "Maybe I'll pop out and frighten the tourists – if I can find some way to disappear afterwards."

That night, after taking a shower, Julie tried on her completed costume. She struggled into the heavy, bone-lined corset, typical of the 1860's. *How in the world did women put these on by themselves?* After pulling on two petticoats, the huge hoop slip, and underskirt, she swayed into her small bathroom, where the hoop filled the tiny, pink room. She parted her long, straight hair neatly in the middle and pulled its lengths back into a bun, using bobby pins to fasten the arrangement at the nape of her neck.

She walked back to the bedroom, lifted the dress over her head, and pushed her arms into the sleeves. Then, she donned the bonnet, throwing the veil up and over the hat to trail down her back. She sashayed to the cheval mirror in the corner of her bedroom and scrutinized herself as she hummed *The Blue Danube*...

The bedside lamp with its low wattage bulb, seemed to enlarge her pupils, making her dark brown irises disappear. Her black hair accentuated her pale, oval face and the small white scar on the corner of her eyelid. She remembered when she was three years old, and how she had attempted to take a bone from her dog.

She lifted her chin and tilted her face so she could see the gross-grain ribbons on her bonnet and tied at her throat. Her tight-fitting basque was trimmed with black braid, while dozens of tiny hooks fastened the blouse close to her body.

She frowned. *Where is my mourning broach?*   And then, she laughed. "But, you didn't buy a pin, you silly!"

* * * *

The Corvair put,-put,-puttered to a stop in the Smith driveway. A bag of McDonald's French fries lay in her lap, along with four cents in change from her quarter, which rattled inside the paper sack. The windshield wipers wagged back and forth to the beat of the music on the local AM station. Julie switched the ignition to the *off* position and sat watching the rain bead, then drip in rivulets down the windshield. She half-hoped the rain would keep tourists away this day, giving her time to indulge her continued fascination with the family...

* * * *

Stephen aimed the nozzle on the hose and sprayed a torrent of water on her. He stood laughing at her shocked expression. They were washing his new Corvair convertible. She looked at Stephen and saw the way the perspiration on his bronzed chest glistened in the sunlight. She shook her head, leaned over, lifted the wide yellow sponge from the bucket and, without warning, threw it at him before he could clear the back end of the car to make his getaway down the driveway of his parent's home. Her slight trim frame allowed her the speed she needed, and she caught the pocket on his jeans, yanked him back, and pulled his face close to hers, then kissed him as the water trickled down their faces. A dog barked...

For just the briefest moment, Stephen was still alive and she was jubilant – and then she remembered. *He's gone, Julie... He's gone forever.*

The early afternoon shower had turned to heavy rain and blew against the parlour window as Julie squinted into the growing darkness. *Who would come out in this weather?* The outline was of a man in a military uniform who brushed at the drops of water beading on his grey wool coat. She turned from the window and hastily smoothed her skirt, patted her hair into place and then hurried to the hall...

* * * *

A black man, clad in butler's garb, opened the door and ushered the guest inside. The soldier stood about five-foot-eight, was solidly built and his hair was a dampened blonde that curled about the collar of his uniform.

Samuel Lightfall turned to Julie. His eyes lighted with pleasure at her countenance. She could feel the erratic beats of her heart and the flush that unexpectedly warmed her face. She looked down at the floor, so the handsome soldier would not see her blush the pleasure of his presence.

The butler stepped between them, blocking Julie's view, and took Samuel's coat; then the servant showed him to the parlour door. "Mayjuh Samuel Lightfall has arrived," the butler announced, and Samuel walked into the parlour, warmed with the glow of apple wood burning in the fireplace, and was lost in the crowd of people who had suddenly filled the room.

A vivacious redheaded girl sat on the gold brocade settee. She fluttered an ostrich feathered fan about her face, unashamedly flirting with a swarthy soldier who held her gloved hand. An ancient-looking woman, dressed in shiny black satin, tickled the chin of a cherubic infant held in his proud mother's arms.

It was a Christmas party. A huge pine tree, nearly reaching the twelve-foot ceiling, was trimmed with ribbon and glass ornaments. A young black woman, dressed in purple with matching head rag, kept a vigilant watch as the flames of the candles on the tree branches snapped and danced in the moving air; a bucket of water by her side. An old man carrying two crystal glasses of punch, squeezed past Julie, crushing her voluminous green velvet gown as he made his way to the pianoforte where a familiar looking woman was playing *We Three Kings*, and who paused only long enough to sip the punch proffered to her.

In an unexpected moment, the crowd parted and Julie saw Samuel speaking with an older, dark-haired woman in a cranberry-colored dress. Julie moved toward them, even as she wondered what she would say to him.

A dog barked and the sound drew her attention. A bell clanged.

"Dennah is served ladies and gempmen!" the butler called out, jangling a large dinner bell.

The dog barked again.

Julie stood up and looked out the window.

* * * *

Only one brave soul had ventured out in the summer storm. Julie turned off the lights, emptied a trash can, and totaled the day's receipts. She then went into the library, sat in the Victorian rocking chair, and leaned her head against its high back. She studied the large engraving that hung over the fireplace, *Daniel Webster Addressing the Senate in 1850.* Behind her, bookcases ran from floor to ceiling, shelving the Smith's prized library of priceless books, some nearly two hundred years old. A lamp burned on the table next to her rocking chair. She opened the book of Caroline's missives and began reading the young wife's letters to her husband.

* * * *

March 17, 1863

My Own,

Spring has arrived and I wish I could rejoice in earth's renewal after such a dismal winter. I realize that with the warmer weather, the armies will be on the move, again. Every step you take away from me brings you ever closer to the enemy - and possible death. I know it is morose of me to dwell on death, but the realization that I am not in a family way makes me very melancholy these days. I will try, my Love, to be more cheerful.

Lizzie says the azaleas should be blooming soon. I look forward to their pretty, pink blossoms. Now that the weather is warmer, I frequently sit near the springhouse, where I find it peaceful and can imagine sitting with you in your surroundings...

The springhouse! That's where Caroline hid Samuel's letters... somewhere around the springhouse! Julie jumped up off the rocking chair and ran for the door; it slammed as she hurried across the porch and down the front steps of the old white house. She grabbed hold of the largest bone hoop at the bottom and, in a very unladylike fashion, lifted it high so her skirting would not get wet and muddied. Her pantalets fluttered as she quick stepped it across the yard to the springhouse about thirty yards from the rise of the hill.

She picked her way carefully around the dripping wet stacked stone springhouse, closely examining the rocks for large crevices that might betray Caroline's hiding place. There were none; nor was there anything unusual about the little structure. She slowly sat down on a large boulder, filled with resignation that it had been a wild goose chase. *Caroline might have sat here,* she thought. *And, if she did, what was she thinking? Was she reading Samuel's letters?* Julie's back stiffened. "So, if I were Caroline sitting here, where would the logical place be to hide the letters," she asked herself, looking around.

A bright green lizard popped out of a crack in the springhouse. His den was about even with Julie's sight line. She leaned forward and peered into the crevice, but a small rock blocked the narrow compartment. She removed the stone and let out a quick gasp; a long and narrow leather folder lay in the small hollow. Her hands shook as she carefully pulled the pouch from the darkness. Tears welled in Julie's eyes as she pressed the cool leather to her cheek, and then she ran back to the house, settled into the rocking chair and, with trembling fingers, carefully untied the near-rotted ribbon and opened the pouch. She lifted the first letter from the small stack, placed it on her knee, and slowly smoothed the creases. Samuel's one-hundred-year-old letters seemed more degraded than Caroline's were but, fortunately, his heavy script was easy to read. "January 7, 1862..."

Dear Miss Barnwell,

I bid you a Happy and Prosperous New Year and pray that 1862 finds our country moving on from this terrible ordeal.

Though it has only been a week since we last met, it feels an eon. The few days we spent together were the most delightful in my life. That I might believe you feel the same way would sustain me during these trying times. I feel you close to me when the men have settled for the night and there is time for private thoughts and quiet reflection.

Your Uncle Archibald was kind to permit me to correspond with you and I will convey my sentiments in a separate letter directly to him.

Miss Barnwell, I wish I could "wax poetic" for you, but this poor soldier is fit only for marching and, God willing, fighting the good fight.

The soldier who has the support of a special fair maiden is truly a lucky man. And, as such, I will try to conduct myself in a manner worthy of your kind attentions.

Your Most Ardent Admirer,
Maj. Samuel Lightfall, CSA

He writes so romantically! He must have fallen in love at first sight... Julie, does it really matter? Get a grip, Julie, she told herself. *God forbid if anyone knew how you really feel about this man whose been gone for a hundred years!* "They'd put you away," she said, lifting Samuel's next letter, and began reading again...

March 5, 1862

Dear Miss Barnwell,

I beg you to excuse the brevity of my words, since this letter must get off to you in a few short minutes.

First, let me say that I am overwhelmed by the number of your generous and informative letters. I am the envy of my men who want to know how their Major has bewitched a young lady into writing every week! I only wish I could return letters to you with the same dedication.

But, I must get to the point!

It is my extreme pleasure to inform you that I will be back in Roswell in a few days. I hope to have the honor of calling on you to pursue the friendship we began last Christmas.

I think of you often and am anxious to see whether my memory serves me right; that you possess the prettiest and deepest brown eyes ever beheld in a woman's face.

You may expect me sometime around 12 March.

> In haste,
> Samuel Lightfall, CSA

It's no wonder Caroline fell in love... how could she not?

April 10, 1862

My Own Caroline,

You are silly to suppose I do not care about the plans for our upcoming nuptials. They are important to you; therefore, I take even the smallest detail very seriously.

The particulars of my leave are still a little vague at this time. As you have scheduled the blessed event for 26 April, I will endeavor to arrive the night before.

I am permitted only five days leave; being a red-blooded man, I prefer to spend the majority of my time in the privacy of our wedding bower. (I wish I could see the blush on your lovely face as you read these bold words.) All bantering aside, I am the most fortunate of men to have won you as my wife. From the first moment I saw you, I knew we would be together the rest of our lives.

This leads to a more serious matter. No doubt, you have heard the dismal news of the battle of Shiloh. The Yankees showed more grit than I supposed they possessed, even if we stampeded them practically into the river. I believe we are in for a longer fight than first supposed.

Caroline, should you decide to postpone our wedding until the end of this war, I would understand. This is not due to reluctance on my part, to marry you, but a practical matter. I am sure your Uncle Archibald would concur.

Believe me to be ever yours,
Samuel

She wiped the tears that flowed more easily. *Oh, Stephen, I'm so glad you wouldn't let me postpone our wedding until you graduated from West Point. I would have had only half the time I did with you... it still hurts so badly I can hardly breathe. I'll always miss you, my love... Always.*

Julie's eyes felt strained from reading the faded, brown ink that Samuel had penned so long ago. There were at least five more letters in the pouch – more than she had first supposed. The mantle clock struck, whirring and clicking its way to six chimes. She shrugged her shoulders and stretched her arms over her head. *I'll take these home and read them... no one will know. I'll show them to Earladene tomorrow.* Julie smiled. *Won't she be excited?*

As she stood up, a sharp tangy scent of bayberry wafted across her face. She took a step and suddenly felt a column of bitter cold air engulfing her – from head-to-toe and from front-to-back. She fell back into the rocking chair, Samuel's letters cascading out of her hand and scattering about the floor.

She reached out, and felt the frosty air. She looked about the room trying to find its source, but could not.

The smell of bayberry grew stronger as it, too, overwhelmed her. She leaned over to gather up the letters and, as she did, a phrase in the topmost portion of one letter caught her eye. She lifted it with a trembling hand.

December 7, 1862

Dearest Caroline,

The cruel cold this winter has caused many of my men to suffer with frostbite... take coats from captured

Yankees... your package, which contained the best ginger cookies ever...and the bayberry pomander takes me back to when we first met at the Christmas party given by your good Aunt and Uncle...

Julie clutched her throat and closed her eyes, then wrapped her arms about her, trying to rationalize what she was experiencing. *It's an old house... there will be drafts. Your imagination has gotten the best of you...*

The bayberry scent dissipated and the air grew warmer. She took a deep breath and slowly exhaled, forcing herself to remain calm. She neatly stacked the letters, taking pains to line-up the edges, and then set the bundle on the floor next to her feet. *Maybe I shouldn't remove them from the house... Maybe Samuel wants me to leave his letters right here...*

Julie closed her eyes. "I must be going crazy. That's it, Julie. You're losing it. *First, it was the picture of Samuel. Then, you had to make a mourning dress. Next thing you know, you'll take up residence in the house.* "I'm calling Earladene to tell her about the letters, and then I'm going home," she said and firmly nodded her head.

Julie looked down at the telephone on the small end table, lifted the black receiver off its cradle and dialed Earladene's phone number. The phone rang, endlessly. She pressed down on the hook and proceeded again, her index finger slipping easily into the holes of the dial.

A breathless Earladene answered. "This better be more important than the heart attack I'm 'bout to have after rushing to the phone," Earladene said through heavy pants and gasps. "Hello... hello! Damn kids!"

Julie placed the receiver down on the cradle. *On second thought, I want to read the rest of Samuel's letters before I tell Earladene.*

Julie took the stained, leather pouch and set it next to her purse. Archibald Smith glared down at her from the library wall. It seemed a disapproving stare.

"I'm only keeping them a secret for a while longer! No harm done," she told the patriarch, and stuck out her tongue.

She moved from room to room, completing her end of the day routines. *It was a draft, that's all. I must have seen a few sentences of that letter, forgot I saw it, and then imagined the smell of bayberry. Maybe I need some time away from here.*

She carried the trash can outside and around the house and emptied the contents into the city dumpster. As she approached the outdoor kitchen with its large fireplace, the smoky smell of burning wood invited her to tarry at the open doorway...

The image of Bettina, tending the fire, suddenly came into Julie's field of vision. She stepped up and into the room where another woman, dressed in a bright orange skirt, stood kneading dough at a well-worn table and at her elbow, stood a child with braids tied with twine. The little girl reached into the bowl and the light-skinned woman promptly slapped her hand. The heat in the room was suffocating and Bettina fanned her face with the end of her large, snowy white apron. Sweat dripped off her broad nose and chin as she lifted the lid from the Dutch oven. Herbs strung up on twine were drying in the hot room; shelves nailed to the kitchen walls held clay bowls, Mason jars and baskets. An apple press stood in the corner, and nearby, hay-lined barrels stood ready to receive sweet, golden bottles of cider. Julie stepped out of the kitchen; she reached for the cut glass knob and pulled the battered door shut behind her.

Satisfied that the premises were secure for the night, Julie threw her purse onto the passenger seat in the Corvair and pulled the black chignon off her head. Her dark locks curled about her face in the humidity. She gathered her skirts in one hand, preparing to slide into the driver's seat, when she glanced up at the second floor bedroom window. A man's face peered down at her. *Who's that? Did I miss him while I was locking up?* "Damn! I want to get home to a cool shower," she said, releasing her skirting and headed for the back door.

* * * *

"Hello, you can't be in here!" Julie called up the stairwell. Silence pressed against her ears. "Hello!"

Julie walked warily up the stairs. She held her car keys in one hand and lifted her skirts out of the way with the other. "I'll call the police!"

At the top of the stairs, she cautiously peered into the bedroom. No one was at the window, but the lace curtain was parted open.

She walked to the window and looked out; robins hopped busily across the soaked lawn, hunting for worms lured to the ground's surface by the rain; two hyperactive squirrels chased each other around the oak tree, and her car door stood open, the dome light illuminating its red interior.

She heard a sliding, creak behind her and turned toward the walnut bureau topped by a crocheted doily. A narrow drawer, which had been ingeniously hidden in the carved façade of the piece, was pulled open. The fragrance of bayberry drifted around her as she went to the open drawer. Inside, resting on a piece of dark stained linen, lay a beautiful pair of tortoise hair combs, the ridges set with small iridescent pearls.

She reached in and gently ran her finger across the pearls on one of the combs and carefully picked it up. *How beautiful!*

She looked at herself in the bureau mirror, its silver backing worn away, mottling and distorting her reflection. She slid first one, then the other comb into her hair which fell loosely down her back.

A shadow moved rapidly from the window, crossing the polished wood floor, to the bureau where Julie stood.

In the upper right corner of the mirror, an image began to take shape, blooming like a pale flower in the dimly-lit room. Her eyes settled on the reflection that slowly transformed into a man's face, and then a torso – clothes that distinguished a Confederate uniform. He filled the mirror as he stood behind her. Their eyes engaged, and in spite of a sense of alarm, Julie could not move or look away from his gaze that held hers. She saw love and tenderness in eyes that drew her deep into their clear blue depths.

His hands gently came to rest on her upper arms and he leaned down, so near to her that his lips were but a kissing breath away. A calming warmth caressed her as she watched Samuel's lips.

"Caroline..."

To be continued...

in Connie's Upcoming Novella

Connie Treloar's Lecture

For those who are interested in the lifestyles of those caught up in the Civil War in Georgia, and of the mysterious and supernatural stories of ghostly sightings and occurrences, you may want to consider scheduling Connie for her lecture, *"They Linger Still."*

Ms. Treloar's knowledge, style and subtle humor have warmed the hearts of hundreds of romantics and history lovers who journey to Roswell, Georgia for just a taste of those long ago days.

It is incumbent upon us to forewarn you: Connie Treloar's passion for the old South—and for those who linger still—will have you questioning what really lies within reality...

For further information, contact:

The Manhattan Group., Inc.
P.O. Box 93
Marietta, GA 30061-0093
Website: www.manhattangroupinc.com
Email: manhattangroup@mindspring.com
Phone/Fax: 678.773.2674

firstWorks' Current Titles

WHORE OF MADNESS
by Dani Dubré

AWESOME WOMEN
*Some Famous... Others Infamous... and
Those Lost in History*
by Leslie "Nicki" Sackrison

LOST IN YESTERDAY
*A 70th Anniversary Commemoration of
Gone With The Wind*
by Peter Bonner

STEPPING ON MEMORIES
A Sister Remembers the Great Depression & WWII
by Marge Griffin-Glausier

Upcoming Titles:

BETRAYED
by Dani Dubré

UNFORGETTABLE
By Connie M. Treloar

Printed in the United States
84863LV00006B/2/A